The Flight into Egypt

A novel by

GRAZIA DELEDDA

Original title: *La fuga in Egitto*, published in 1926
Translated from the Italian by Kevan Houser

ISBN 978-1-64970-346-0

Dedication

Like all my translations, this is dedicated to the countless Italians and Italophiles who have contributed to my understanding of—and love for—the Italian language and culture over the past many years.

You are all appreciated.

I feel indebted to everyone who has graciously shared this beautiful, expressive language with me. Bringing work by Italian writers, including this Grazia Deledda novel, back into the light of day represents a tiny step towards repaying that debt. My hope is that providing a new English translation of this engaging work, beyond opening a fascinating door to a distant time and place for today's English-language reader, contributes in some small way to further promoting Italian literature to a worldwide Anglophone audience.

Grazie a tutti — Thank you all, and thank you to my family and friends for the moral support along the way.

Yes, you can contact me! I'm always glad to hear from you!

Send email to: envoyfeedback@yahoo.com

Let me know what you like and don't like about this work and my translation. Also welcome are suggestions for future translations, particularly Italian works in the public domain that either have never been translated into English, or perhaps have existing translations which are out of print or outdated.

Finally, if you enjoy this work, **please leave feedback on Amazon and/or Goodreads**. Reviews are crucial to helping bring attention to a book.

Contents

Introduction..9

Who was Grazia Deledda?....................................11

Part I - The Family..17

Part II - The Sin..89

Part III - The Penance...125

Part IV - The Birth..221

Part V - The Flight..259

From the Translator's Notebook..........................267

About the Translator / Other Books Available...................281

Introduction

As I learn more about Grazia Deledda and read more of her work, I have to wonder if she's relatively unknown in the English-speaking world because so few of her novels have been translated, or if so few of her novels have been translated because she's relatively unknown?

It's something of a catch-22 after all—how can people come to know and appreciate an author if they can't read most of her work? But on the other hand, why would someone invest the time and effort into translating a 100-year-old novel into English that people haven't heard of and aren't clamoring to read?

I did it because I have the time and energy, but more importantly, because I believe that Deledda's voice is one that deserves to heard by more people. And, as I say in the dedication, contributing to the promotion of Italian literature is something of a mission for me.

I "discovered" Grazia Deledda by chance, through a used copy of the Italian edition of *Elias Portolu* that happened to appear at Powell's Bookstore. I was amazed to learn that such a significant work by a Nobel Laureate in literature was all but impossible to find in English (a translation done a quarter century ago was long out of print), and so I decided to translate and publish a new version myself.

In fact, of Deledda's approximately 40 novels, perhaps four or five are currently available in English. Case in point is *The Flight into Egypt,* first published in 1926. I can find no evidence of an English translation ever being commercially available (there is, however, a German edition listed on Amazon). I found *Flight* to be quite different from *Elias*: more modern, certainly, but also more confidently written, definitely a more mature work. The two novels do, however, share a related theme: sin and redemption. They also share Deledda's keen ability as an observer of both people and nature.

This new translation of *The Flight into Egypt* thus adds to the breadth of Deledda's work available to the English-speaking public, and it is my hope that it will likewise add to an understanding and appreciation of the prolific Sardinian author as well.

Who Was Grazia Deledda?

Few Italian women writers achieved widespread recognition in the early twentieth century, and none to the degree of the humble, middle-class Deledda, who would go on to become the first (and so far, only) Italian woman to win the Nobel Prize for Literature, doing so in 1926, that is, the same year this novel you hold in your hands was first published. In the words of the Nobel citation, Deledda was recognized "for her idealistically inspired writings, which with plastic clarity picture the life on her native island and with depth and sympathy deal with human problems in general."

Grazia Maria Cosima Damiana Deledda was born on September 27, 1871, just one year after Italy's final unification and two months after the capital was officially moved from Florence to Rome. But her native village on Sardinia, the second-largest Mediterranean island, must have seemed a world away from the action and turmoil on the continent. (Interestingly, Deledda reportedly never even saw the sea until as a teenager she rode a horse to Mount Bardia, from where she could finally glimpse the Mediterranean.) Nuoro was a town of about 5,500 inhabitants when Deledda entered the world, the fourth of seven children (according to her Italian Wikipedia page; some sources offer varying numbers) born to respectable, bourgeois parents. Her father, Giovanni Antonio

Deledda, was a miller, a landowner, a self-published poet, and, among other things, briefly mayor. Perhaps most important to Grazia's future career was his extensive collection of books.

Despite their relatively fortunate position, life for young Grazia in Nuoro (which she once called "a bronze-age village") was far from idyllic, however. Island winters were harsh (a subject she touches on in *Elias Portolu*), food was scarce at times, and the deadly cold claimed a young sister of hers who perished in bed one winter when the Deledda house was entirely barricaded by snow. Grazia experienced other tragedies as well: a second sister also died in bed, covered in blood following a miscarriage. Deledda washed that sister's body and dressed her in white (another experience reflected in *Elias Portolu*). Deledda's brothers added to the family drama and tragedy. One stole money from them to finance visits to bordellos throughout the Mediterranean. Another's life fell apart when he began drinking heavily after his face was burned in a fireworks accident.

Young Grazia's education began early, when her maternal uncle, a clergyman named Sebastiano Cambosu, taught her to read and write before she began her formal education, which ended abruptly at age eleven, when she'd completed the four years deemed appropriate for girls at the time. After that, she was briefly home schooled by a private tutor, and after he disappeared, she undertook an independent study of Italian, Russian, French, and English literature, along with Sardinian legends and folklore. Interestingly, her mother tongue wasn't

Italian, but Logudorese Sardo (*il sardo logudorese),* a variant or dialect of Sardinian. (That was the only language that her mother, Francesca Cambosu, spoke, and the language that her father used to write poetry.) The standard Italian in which Deledda so poignantly wrote was, in effect, a "foreign" language.

She began writing at a young age, with some shorter works appearing in local newspapers and magazines around 1890 (sources vary), much to the chagrin of the people of Nuoro. Seeing themselves unflatteringly reflected in her writing, they were scandalized. Infuriated townspeople burned copies of the magazine *L'Ultima moda* when it published one of her stories (about a love triangle) in 1890, deeming it shocking and unseemly. Her first successful novel, *Fiori di Sardegna* ("Flowers of Sardinia"), inspired by the people and land she so intimately knew, and the harsh realities Sardinian peasants struggled with, was published in 1892 and sold well on the Italian mainland, but the closest bookstore, the one she'd patronized her entire life and which was instrumental to the writer's self-education, refused to carry copies of it. The rigid, patriarchal society simply didn't approve of her work, and Deledda was initially infamous on her native island and endured harsh criticism for daring to so boldly depict some of Sardinia's pagan customs and beliefs.

Despite all that, she persisted, as we might say in modern parlance. She continued writing with insight and sympathy about her homeland, its people, and their challenges, even after marrying (Palmiro Madesani, a civil servant, in 1900) and relocating to Rome, where she had two sons (Sardus and Franz) and lived for the rest of her life. Never judging nor condemning her characters, she frequently addressed the interplay of Christianity and pagan superstition in forming the moral compass that governed her isolated, agricultural birthplace. Her writing draws the reader into her characters' anguish as they struggle to abide by those almost sacred rules, yet inevitability end up breaking them. The crushing emotional weight of their guilt and sin is counterbalanced by an innocent longing for expiation and redemption.

This theme of transgression, with a tragically flawed main character torn between right and wrong, hope and despair, mortal sin and divine redemption takes center stage in *Elias Portolu*, which was published in 1903, and might be considered her breakthrough success, marking her arrival as a successful, internationally known writer. Numerous novels followed, including *Cenere* ("Ashes") in 1904, which inspired a silent movie featuring famous Italian stage actress Eleonora Giulia Amalia Duse ("Duse" as she was popularly known, a contemporary and longtime rival of Sandra Bernhard) who came out of retirement for her sole film role. Deledda's most well-known book in Italy was probably 1913's *Canne al vento* ("Reeds in the Wind") or 1918's *L'incendio nell'oliveto* ("The Fire in the Olive Grove").

It's widely reported that upon learning she'd won the prestigious Nobel, the white-haired, five-foot-tall woman simply exclaimed *Gia!* (Already!) and promptly returned to her desk, maintaining her strict writing schedule and doting on her pet crow, Checcha. Over her working life, that dedication enabled her to produce around 40 novels (sources report various numbers) and a considerable collection of short stories. Although most well-known for her prose, she was prolific in a number of other areas as well, writing poetry, essays, theatrical plays, an opera libretto, articles on folklore, and children's stories, as well as translating works such as Balzac's *Eugénie Grandet*.

Remarkably, little of her overall contribution to world literature is known to English-speaking audiences today, with only a small portion even having been translated.

In 1936, at the age of 64, Deledda died in Rome of breast cancer. She was laid to rest in the velvet maroon dress she had worn in Stockholm ten years earlier, delivering one of the briefest acceptance speeches in Nobel Prize history. Her remains lie in Sardinia, at the foot of Mount Ortobene (a mountain mentioned in *Elias Portolu*), where a church was built in her honor. Her birthplace and childhood home in Nuoro has also been preserved as a museum (Museo Deleddiano di Nuoro), with its ten rooms depicting various stages of the author's life.

In 1985, a 32-kilometer crater on the planet Venus was named in her honor by the International Astronomical Union's (IAU) Working Group for Planetary System Nomenclature.

The great Russian writer Maksim Gorky had this to say about her: "What pens and what strong voices! She has no rivals neither in the present nor in the past."

English writer and poet D.H. Lawrence commented: "Grazia Deledda has an island all for herself, Sardinia, especially the mountain range where live the people which she feels the charm of."

Finally, Deledda once described herself thus: *"I'm very small, you know, I'm short even compared to Sardinian women who are very small, but I'm bold and brave like a giant and I'm not afraid of intellectual battles."*

Part I

The Family

1.

After forty years as an elementary school teacher, Giuseppe De Nicola had retired and was getting ready to go on a journey.

Here's the background: As a young man he had adopted an orphan boy, hoping he would one day take over for him at the school in his little hometown. The boy, however, preferred an adventurous life, so he ran away from home, and after having attempted every trade from sailor to port laborer, from chamois hunter to customs guard, he'd ended up meeting and marrying the widow of a boat owner whose inheritance consisted of a large house on the Adriatic shore with its attendant vineyards and farmland.

Having finally found a suitable situation, the young man sent his adoptive father a box of cigars, a remnant of his turbulent past, named his first child Giuseppina Nicola after him, and eventually invited him, on behalf of his wife as well, to come live with them.

And the teacher, down there in his damp little town amid mountains and valleys in the middle of nowhere, thought about this new family, about this marvelous seaside setting, and intended to embark on a voyage to visit them, like one of the Magi off to Bethlehem. But the distance scared him, as did the railway strikes then frequent and the five transfers required to arrive at that dream town.

And so, a few years passed, until he retired. Finding himself alone, without even his rowdy, thankless school family, he

18

made up his mind to finally embark on the great voyage. Indeed, he left with a religious joy, but not without a vague sense of terror.

It was his first journey, that trip, his honeymoon with life. Not even his young son, fleeing the confining walls of his family home in search of space and fortune, had taken such a flying leap from reality to dream. The ground disappeared from under his feet like a shiny ballroom floor. Nature danced around him, the cloaks of the constantly changing landscape folding and unfolding before him, dragging him along, so high up the mountains he could touch the clouds, inside tunnels, black and smoky like chimney pipes, out over the dizzying blueness of rivers, and down along green slopes where it felt like he was rolling naked on cold grass.

He was clinging to the window of the train car, one filled with traveling children, and when they plummeted into the blackness of the tunnels, he would pull his head back in, afraid it would be cut off in that enigma by a roaming monster. With the first glimmer of light, he would stick it back out, oblivious to how the train's wind was happily dancing with violence in his gray hair and filling his nose with soot.

A newlywed couple, arm in arm next to the other window, watched the world fly by in each other's eyes. He wasn't jealous of them since they were all headed to the same destination together.

2.

His first disappointment was waiting for him on arrival, when the train stopped in the little station and big, smiling poplars were bowing left and right to greet travelers, but there was no one to meet him.

He was afraid he'd gotten mixed up. He was the only one to get off the train, which was already pulling away, whistling, as if at him. The stillness of the vineyards in that suddenly immobile landscape, the bushes seemingly filled with sleeping butterflies, the blades of grass hunching over their own long, lively shadows provoked a febrile stupor in him. Amidst all that green, only the red roof of the station stood out. Outside the station he waited, standing up straight between his two suitcases like the shaft of a balance scale, but all he saw before him was a broad grassy boulevard with a giant egg—half blue sea and half sky—at the end.

Above the boulevard, between the two rows of poplar and locust trees that looked like married couples—the tall, slender poplars and the short, rounded locusts, covered with shimmering foliage—the sky was high and clear, but with an inexpressible sadness, all the sadder because it made no sense. It was the sadness of a great solitude, not in the sky, but in the heart of the man looking at it.

And the man with the suitcases had the impression of having disembarked somewhere worse than a boundless city where no one spoke his language, and if he were to walk, he'd have to walk a long way just to reach a deserted beach.

He was suddenly gripped by a wistful longing for his little house far away. Why had he left his old home and the town where his relatives were buried, where he still had some friends?

Like the young and the weak who don't know the joy of solitude, he'd allowed himself to be deceived by the blue off in the distance. He thought he'd packed only life's necessities in those two suitcases whose new leather scent revealed their bearer was a novice traveler. But life takes its revenge, and now those suitcases were weighing him down as if crammed full of his entire past.

And more than ever, he felt the insurmountable distance that separated him from the family that, in the end, wasn't his.

A family is created by a man with his very own essence, with his seed, his blood, his sweat. But the only sentimental bond between him and that other family was more fragile than a spider's thread.

So much so that no one came to meet him.

3.

But he didn't even consider turning back. In fact, he set out calmly walking along the long boulevard, immediately consoling himself with the hope that tomorrow and beyond his own solitude could be accompanied by that of the peaceful walk.

"We'll be friends, my fine road. After all, you've greeted me warmly—you're the only one who came to meet me and you're keeping me company."

The road, in fact, treated him better and better, soft with fine, fragrant grass, and through the arches between one tree and the next, he caught glimpses of tranquil fields with white cows and black horses at pasture, the farmers' houses repainted ochre and pink, the flowering bushes, and the gleaming pergolas—everything as colorful as a picture postcard.

Behind the tree trunks, gentian flowers seemingly waited to ambush him, swaying as he passed by. Even the tenuous voice of the sea reached him now, like that of a friend, even though he and the sea, whom he hadn't yet met, shared a misunderstanding born of fear and loathing.

It was from that turquoise wall of gentian in fact, growing taller before him, that the first two human figures appeared, giving him hope that he hadn't gotten lost, or at least that they could help him find the right way, especially since they were approaching him, looking at his suitcases as if they were extraordinary items.

He quickened his pace and his heart filled with light.

Maybe it was his little granddaughter, the dark-haired girl dressed in red whose hand the other figure, a young woman, was holding. It really was his granddaughter.

"Would you be the schoolteacher, Mr. De Nicola?" the woman asked with a manly voice, coming to a halt like a soldier in front of him. "Your son had to leave unexpectedly on urgent business, and his wife is in bed with a fever that comes on every three days. — Say hello to your grandfather, Ola. — Give me your suitcases."

Ola looked her grandfather up and down. After her black, slanting eyes brimming with glimmers of gold had taken in his entire person, absorbing its every detail, she didn't seem inclined to say a thing. Instead, she stepped back, taking hold of the hem of her little dress. And yet, in that ruffled dress spreading out in her hands like a poppy plucked from the stem, and in that stiff little figure, and above all, in that golden face tilted back amidst her flowering black curls, an irresistible offer resonated.

Letting go of his suitcases like so much dead weight, the grandfather took her in his arms, feeling her warm and alive against him. And when her hair, which was salty, and her cheek, softer and smoother than velvet, grazed his mouth, he started, as if touched by love.

Meanwhile, the woman had taken the suitcases and was on her way, swinging them like two light purses. So tall and well-built, she was a young Juno, crowned with yellow braids.

The schoolteacher followed her, carrying his new weight.

"So, your name is Ola. I've known that for a while now. Ola…"

The sweet name melted in his mouth like a honeyberry.

Ola delicately shied away, but willingly let herself be carried, without taking her unsettled eyes, filled with sunshine and shadows, off his face. It was a studious glance more than anything else, taking in the wrinkles of that face, so near and yet so unfamiliar, the black spots on the nose, his black and white hairs in close company like night and day. And her gaze penetrated his mouth, trying to explain the mystery of the gold teeth hiding there in the back like her mom's rings in the dresser drawer. She didn't say a thing, though, and to his many questions she finally replied evasively:

"Daddy's bringing me a shotgun today."

"A shotgun? But shotguns are for boys. Do you know what I brought you? A nice doll."

"I have dolls," she said, greeting the news with indifference. Then she put her tiny finger on his tie pin, which she'd already examined carefully, her eyes gleaming with desire. "Daddy has one too, with a little red stone, but he doesn't want to give it to me."

"Now we're making progress. You'd like to have this? Well then, if I give it to you, what would you give me in return?"

Ola lowered her head, and then slowly, slowly lifted it back up and kissed him on the cheek.

"Oh, you little rascal, you already have a knack for it. Well then, the pin is yours, but I'll give it to you when we get home."

Then red with delight, she surrendered into his arms. And they were immediately friends.

When they arrived at the bend in the boulevard, the road became less generous, a path actually, furrowed by the passage of carts, so the woman advised the teacher to put the girl down.

"That one there, she'll take advantage of anything if you let her. Down, Ola, your grandfather is tired."

"I'm tired too," she replied, her voice honestly sounding tired. And she didn't take her finger off the little stone on the pin—that was what mattered to her.

"Just a bit more," said the grandfather, hugging her closer as if afraid of losing her. And he did it in such a way that the big, annoying girl went on ahead.

"Who is that?" he asked when he thought she couldn't hear. "Is she the servant?"

"She's Ornella," said Ola.

"*Ornella*. It's a fine name. But does she live with you?"

"Yes. She's the cousin of the daddy who died before my daddy, and she does everything at home."

"Oh, I see. She's a poor relative."

Then they talked about more important things. Over the hedge to the right of the path, between the ashen tamarisks, appeared the intense blue of the sea, and Ola turned that direction to look, somewhat captivated.

"Who makes all that water?" she asked softly, absorbed in that great mystery.

"Oh, we'll have time to answer that!" he exclaimed loudly, suddenly seeing the emptiness of his idle days filling up like the horizon of the sea.

"Don't you go to school?"

"Me? No. I'm still too little."

"That's all right, I'll bring school to you. We'll go to the beach, and I'll tell you who makes all that water."

25

But she already had a dislike for school and mentioned that there are seashells on the beach—instead of studying, it'd certainly be better to collect seashells. She even liked gathering little flowers, and seeing a trembling row of them on the grass of the path, she asked her grandfather to set her down. First, though, touching the pin again, she wanted to say something in strict confidence.

"Don't tell anyone that you're giving it to me."

He'd never heard a more delicious secret to keep, and the breath from that sweet-smelling mouth opened his ears like fresh lavender oil.

How many secrets would follow that one?

A second one in fact followed immediately after he declared, as a way of enhancing the value of his gift, that the pin was made of gold.

Ola quickly glanced at the woman, crinkled her nose mischievously, and with an air of derision and doubt regarding his claim, whispered in his ear:

"Gold? That stuff that a Moor poops?"

That dirty word was the funniest thing in the world for both of them. They both laughed out loud, looking at the servant's formidable back, and were now partners in crime.

And with that laughter, he felt all the years since his childhood melt away, taking him back to where he'd started, to man's instinctual happiness, the only true happiness. And the meadows, the beach, the paths through the tamarisks, and every nook and cranny of the joyous landscape smiled upon him like a little boy who had finally found a companion to enjoy them all with.

4.

Ornella came to a halt at an iron gate painted bright red, set the suitcases on the ground, and opened the latch.

The schoolteacher and Ola made their way slowly, chatting—she looking up, he with his head lowered to better hear—and they noticed nothing else, so much so that when his eyes did lift and he somewhat dreamily saw the woman and the gate, he thought it would burn him. And perhaps as a contrast to that fiery red and the golden pomegranate red of the house visible at the end of the pathway, the garden where they entered seemed to have been planted on a dry riverbed. In reality, the ground was white and sandy, and the trees were pale and silvery like a watery reflection.

Against this faded backdrop, the porcelain hues of the purple irises and red roses stuck out with exasperation.

Two large terraces with balustrades protruded from the upper façade of the house, but on the ground floor stood a small porch with a stucco floor and columns covered with climbing roses that surrounded the main entrance. Everything was clean and pretty, and the teacher felt a mix of gratification and awe thinking that this distinguished property belonged to his daughter-in-law, and thus to his son as well. However, he noticed all the closed windows facing the splendor of the sea, giving the impression that the house was dark and uninhabited inside.

Indeed, Ornella didn't head for the porch, but turned along the side of the building and when she was behind the house, she pushed open a little door, revealing the backdrop of a kitchen. A pergola crammed with figs and vines set against the walls of the house obscured the entire ground floor. With no apologies, the servant ushered the guest into the shadowy kitchen from where he saw the shadowy adjoining room. He felt new disappointment in this cold, humble reception by a house that was striking only on the outside, like a beautiful woman freshly made up and smiling, but heartless.

But the girl immediately comforted him, touching and tapping her fingernail on the turquoise pot simmering with a good aroma on the damp, steam-covered stove.

"There's a chicken in here. Do you want to see?"

"Stop with the nonsense," said the woman, shoving her forward, between the two suitcases, a bit roughly with her knee.

The teacher didn't like that—neither that nor the semi-darkness of the little dining room that they passed through to get to another room, small as well, sad and almost entirely occupied by a large wooden bed whose green cover enhanced the pallor of the woman lying there. She lifted her head amidst a wave of frizzy black hair and stared with misty, frightened eyes at the man bowing to greet her. It seemed she didn't remember that he was supposed to arrive, or that she thought she was the one who had come from far away to stay with people she didn't know.

The girl, whose face had sharpened and turned serious, jumped on the other side of the bed hollering:

"Momma, it's Grandfather! Grandfather has arrived!"

"Yes, yes, I know," said the woman, annoyed. She closed and reopened her eyes as if to gather up her bewildered expression and replace it with a more alert one. But she acted like someone exhausted and unable to stay awake.

She closed her eyes once more and pulled her bare, white, veinless arms from the sheets, reaching her hands out to the teacher.

He took those hands, oddly large and dark, capping off slender arms, and felt their strong trembling. But one was closed, holding something, and he immediately let it go. The arm dropped and the hand opened a bit, revealing beads from a small mother-of-pearl rosary.

That made him think.

"How are you doing?" he asked softly, his tone immediately paternal. "Isn't it possible to break these fevers?"

"I've had them for ten years. It's malaria, and there's no remedy. Adelmo tried everything to cure me. He even sent for a powder from the Indies. He even went to a psychic, my Adelmo."

Adelmo had been her first husband, and the teacher noticed that her voice had a dreamlike quality as she distinctly enunciated his name the way children do with new words they like because for them, words embody a whole new world of mysterious feelings. He realized that in her febrile state she was reliving the past, and he hesitated to further intrude on that intimacy that belonged to her alone.

But guessing his thoughts from the way he set her hand back on the sheet, she tried to wake up better. Her eyes opened wide, almost with malice, and she cleared her throat.

"You must excuse me for not having come to the station. Tomorrow you'll see that I'm a different woman. Antonio also asked me to convey his apologies. He's such a good man, too. Now go wash up and eat. Go."

He obeyed. When they were in the little dining room where Ornella had set the suitcases down, the girl opened the cupboard drawer, attempting to pull out the tablecloth. She wanted to set the table herself, for her grandfather, but again the woman pushed her aside with her knee.

Then, a bit harshly, he said: "Let her do it. She needs to learn anyway."

The woman didn't reply. She just looked down on him with those placid greenish eyes—a calm gaze that nevertheless informed him that in that household, she was the boss.

"Please follow me to your room," she said after a moment, taking the suitcases. And he saw that the room assigned to him was the gloomiest of all. Moisture stains decorated the walls with strange yellow designs, and on the cracked floor, in the greenish semi-darkness, he thought he saw a cockroach scurry by. But next to the door Ola looked on, self-conscious

30

and curious, and her little red dress illuminated the room like a wintertime fire.

"You can come in, young lady," he said, kneeling. And with one hand he offered her a box, and with the other, between his thumb and index finger, the golden pin he'd taken from his necktie. Ola stepped forward, slowly and cautiously. She took the gifts in silence, with indifference, instead keeping her eyes fixed on the chaos of the opened suitcases, and the entire world still unknown to her within. And to prevent that world from being denied her, her little mind came up with the idea of promising her grandfather something in return:

"I'll take you to see the hens and the little colt."

He would have preferred to see the house first. In fact, after they had eaten and Ornella went to wash some clothes in the fountain next to the tenant farmers' house, he asked if the keys hanging next to the dining room door were for the upper floors.

"Yes, but Daddy doesn't want anyone touching them," she said, vexed, seeing him taking the keys down. For a moment, her proprietary instinct brought on a hostile, almost menacing expression, and then she found a way to smooth things over: "You're Daddy's boss since he's your son, right? He can't scold you."

He held his index finger to his mouth, and they went. She was walking on tiptoes, the doll with the brick-red wool hair that he'd brought her slumped over her shoulder. She guided

31

him, showing him which key opened the main door and which were for the individual apartments.

Then it was as if they'd stepped into an enchanted house. The floor was shiny, with pink, yellow, and turquoise tiles, and the staircase was marble. The stucco walls were decorated with festoons, flowers, and fruit—all in bad taste, but wonderful in Ola's eyes, and maybe in her grandfather's as well. She would look at things and then look at him, and seeing him nodding his head in approval and shaking his hand to say *these are really swanky*, she would clench her little teeth to keep from giggling with joy.

"The light, the light!" she whispered, and he turned it on. The electric light made things brighter, and she went up, rubbing against the walls like a kitten, while the doll's birdlike eyes looked on as well, furtively and with amazement, through the bangs of its barbaric hairdo.

"Every year a count comes here," Ola said, in front of the recently painted door to the second floor, and she drew a little closer to her grandfather, uneasy, as if the noble lodger was there inside. They turned the light on in there too, and the floor, the gilding, and the women's faces painted on the headboards came to life and took on color. Then, when the light went off, they went black again and seemed to go into hiding.

She enjoyed that game and asked her grandfather to turn the light on and off. Although she'd only been in the apartment a few times, she knew every item inside out and quietly pointed them out to him. She didn't touch anything, however, and tried not to brush against the furniture, not even with her dress.

The apartment was rented all year to the count, who came with his family for swimming season and sometimes in the spring too. The third floor, more modest, with simple but new furnishings and upside-down mattresses that reeked of mothballs, was only rented out in the summer.

And yet Ola liked it better and was more familiar with it because she was always let in and well received by the families with children who usually came to stay there.

"Then here, there's something else!" she said to her grandfather, pushing him towards the door of the sitting room.

In the sitting room itself, the light wasn't working. She went in anyway, guided by the light from the hall, pulling her grandfather along to the corner next to the terrace shutter.

"Look here, but don't touch," she said, still whispering.

He bent over to see better. Sitting on a little armchair was a ragdoll dressed in blue. Her eyes, blonde hair, nose, and mouth were painted on the fabric, but still appeared realistic. In fact, the grandfather thought that the lips, a bit raised on one side, were moving in amusement, and that there was something alive and evil about the entire doll.

"Did it scare you?" asked Ola, teasing him. Then she said reassuringly: "It's just a doll, like this one."

Holding her own doll, she lowered it with maternal attention towards the other, making the two mysterious

33

creatures kiss. All this amused her so much that the laughter that had for so long been locked away in her mouth spurted out from her clenched little teeth the way spring water bursts through rocks. Then the grandfather felt that sort of fawning enchantment that was spurring them to wander the house like thieves melt away. After all, it was Ola's house. And it seemed like she and the two dolls were cheerfully mocking him.

"This is your house," he said defiantly. "Let's hope that when you're grown up, you'll enjoy it."

Then he suddenly opened the terrace shutter and the room filled with all the blue from the sea and fiery glimmers of the red sails on the horizon.

5.

Towards evening the malarial woman felt her fever break. It was like the onslaught of cool air on a summer night, and the sweat that dampened her burning skin felt like dew. Even her black hair, which during the fever seemed like a scorching-hot burden, grew lighter, almost evaporating like a cloud strewn and dissolved by the wind.

Along with a sense of reality, she regained a joy of living. The two days separating her from the fever's next assault seemed like two years to her, and she planned to live them the way a convalescent would a long period of health. Everything was fresh and light. Even her little girl, instinctively recognizing that moment of happiness and taking advantage of it to run wild around the room, seemed more beautiful, more alive to her.

Remembering that her father-in-law had come to live with them brought her joy as well—finally she had someone to unburden herself to.

"Where's your grandfather?" she asked the girl.

"He's out there, smoking a pipe."

"Him too!" she groaned, knowing from experience that for men both young and old, the pipe was a woman's formidable rival.

"But he doesn't fling the ash all over, even on plates like Daddy does. He wraps it up in a little package and says it's good for killing ants."

"Tell him to come here, please. And keep an eye out that no one goes in the kitchen until Ornella comes out."

The girl couldn't have been happier, because when Ornella was alone in the kitchen, she would knead dough for focaccia or set a potato in the hot ashes to cook. Then whatever happened, happened.

Still bathed in the scent of strong tobacco, the grandfather entered the woman's room alone, and when she asked him if he had been bored or if the girl had upset him, he emphatically replied:

"This is one of the best days of my life!"

"If this first day was good, the others will be better still," she said cordially. "Have a seat there for a moment if it's not a bother. I'm fine now. Tomorrow I'll be totally recovered and

I'll see to everything myself. Ornella is able and careful, but she's nothing like the mistress of a household."

The teacher sat next to the big bed whose green cover in the dying light from the little window blocked by the garden foliage gave the impression of a lawn at dusk.

There were many questions he wanted to ask his daughter-in-law, and he was glad that she had approached him of her own accord, but her deep, rich voice which also possessed something of a hollow tone, immediately stirred a sense of mystery in him.

Even her figure appeared strange to him—long and barely outlined under the cover in which she was bundled up to her chin, with her beautiful white and black head sunk so far into the pillow that it seemed painted on.

"I'm glad that you're happy here," she continued without looking at him. "We've wanted to have you here with us for so long. Not a day goes by that your son doesn't speak of you with affection and devotion, constantly regretting the grief he's caused you."

"What grief!"

"Then it doesn't bother you that he didn't follow your desire to study, to at least earn a diploma? He decided to try every job, when with his intelligence, who knows what he could have achieved. True, then perhaps he and I never would have met," she observed, her voice even softer, "and our little girl wouldn't be here. I can no longer conceive of a world without our beautiful little girl. And when he complains and regrets not following his father's advice, that's what I tell him. Then he looks at the girl and doesn't say a word, but his eyes brighten like he wants to cry."

She continued, louder. "Besides, we're happy this way. Perhaps too happy. It even scares me. Antonio is kind, cheerful, affectionate. His only vice is smoking—his pipe is in use starting first thing in the morning, and wherever he goes, all I do is clean up ashes and used matches. But you know, a good wife has many duties. I wish that was all there was to it! Then I have to make amends for this ailment, for being up one day and in bed three. I realize I brought it on myself from loving my first husband too much. You know he was a long-time captain and owned his own boats, my poor Adelmo. Once we were married, I wanted to follow him everywhere, in part because I was insanely jealous. I went with him all the way to Porto Corvo, where the whole town was decimated by malaria. But my jealousy blinded me to any danger except that of being justified. Adelmo would say to me, 'What you have is a sin, and God will punish you.' And God did punish me. And the days when I have the fever, I feel like he's still alive and saying, 'See, now if I want to sin with some other woman, you can't chase after me anymore.' And I suffer enormously because I feel like he really is betraying me."

"Did he die young?" asked the teacher, himself a bit jealous on behalf of his son on account of this strange rival.

"He wasn't terribly young, but he looked it. But let's not talk about that anymore. It was so long ago," she murmured, closing her eyes as if to stop seeing the past, or better, to hide her still vivid passion. "Then for a few years the fevers seemed to disappear. Now, since last summer, they've been plaguing me again. Well, as I was saying, your son is so kind and patient, and he searches for any remedy to cure me, and other than the pipe, he has no vices. He just likes a few good drinks, but who doesn't like a nice glass of wine?"

"Me, for example. I'm a teetotaler."

The woman lowered her eyelids and looked at him with cunning and compassion.

"I've never met a man who didn't drink wine, and very few women at that. Everyone here works, and we don't have theaters or other entertainment. Life is hard and the only remedy is a good glass of wine."

"But you have a good income."

"By dint of our hard work, exactly. The earth is thankless, the sea unreliable, and the farmers and fishermen collude to grab the lion's share. Poor Adelmo knew them well, those people, and so he was able to manage them, especially the sea scoundrels, as he called them. He'd been traveling since he was a little boy, all the way to the Indies and Australia, and he used to say that seaports are like glasses of milk and wine—they attract all the most tainted flies. Antonio, though—" After a brief pause that invariably separated the memory of her dead husband from that of the living one, as though disconnecting from the past left a gap in her mind, she continued: "Antonio is more unassuming. He's seen the world too, but never got to know people. He traveled around like a boy with money in his pocket running away from home, having fun. In the early days after we were married, everyone cheated him—or rather, they cheated us because I wasn't very experienced either. Later on we learned the hard way. Besides, he used to love having a good time. He would go dancing every night, and during the day too. I was never jealous with him, but to tell the truth, I went through some rough times because of women."

The teacher laughed very, very softly. Antonio didn't have vices: wine, tobacco, and women were simply things that a man of the world can't avoid.

"Then, seeing that things were going downhill, he came to his senses. I have to say though, that he was respectful and humble with me, even through the darkest moments. When a man admits his errors and promises to turn over a new leaf, what can you do? Maybe close one eye if he doesn't keep his promises, especially if someone you have to hide human weakness from is caught in the middle."

"You talk like a saint," exclaimed the teacher. "And now…"

"Now…" she paused, already regretting having spoken too much. "Everything's going well. Antonio keeps an eye on the farmers and wrestles with the fishermen. Just today he went to Porto Corvo because he learned that the men are unloading poached fish down there."

"How many boats do you have?"

"Four, now. Poor Adelmo had managed to assemble six of them, like a team of horses. The income is good, but the expenses and taxes are high. The same goes for the house—the sea wind has teeth like a wolf."

"And you live here…" he said, looking around at the small, sad, ground-floor room, but the woman didn't even seem to comprehend that she could live, at least part of the year, in the beautiful rooms of the house.

"It's nice here. There're no stairs to deal with. Before building this house, poor Adelmo and I lived in a single room, in town."

"But yet, you were happier."

"Oh, no. We were young, so we were tougher."

"But you're still young," said the teacher, looking at her innocent profile gleaming almost silvery against the dense black thicket of her hair. And she smiled to confirm his statement, revealing unblemished teeth, but it was a slightly bitter smile.

"I'm fifteen years older than your Antonio… That's another reason… I'm not as young as I was back then."

She took her smile back, hiding her teeth, the way one takes back and hides a jewel after having barely shown it. Then the teacher leaned towards her with his hands clasped and whispered:

"Besides, you didn't have the girl, back then."

And they both fell silent as if in prayer.

The little girl's spirit hovered about, spreading a sense of religious mystery in the bleakness of the room where things grew black and the window went blind.

An indefinable instinct told the teacher that the woman, beneath the surface of her desired and even believed happiness, concealed a heartfelt pain that didn't stop when the fever did. She in turn understood his premonition, and they each wanted to confide in the other, but couldn't.

The girl's spirit spun a web around them, more luminous and fragile than a spider's web around a bush, and it drew them together, but at the same time it prevented them from pronouncing a single word that might disperse her work. They had to keep silent for her sake. For her sake, not even a breath could be allowed to disrupt the atmosphere.

"An illusion, perhaps," thought the teacher. But he knew that illusion was the blood of the human spirit.

And since their silence began taking on a hint of anguish, and words were trying to gush out like a violent element, the girl took care of breaking and casting light on it herself, by tapping her fingernails on the glass outside the window. Her little red dress ignited the gray shadows, dispelling them, and her smile reawakened their life forces.

6.

It was already night and the master of the house hadn't returned. Ola and her grandfather sat next to the kitchen door waiting for him while Ornella, after taking some food to the sick woman, was frying something on the stove.

The teacher would turn every so often to look at her, almost unintentionally, with an instinctive expression like the one his granddaughter directed at things and people she didn't know yet. With the already developed curves of a thirty-year-old woman, slightly harsh blonde braids like mature spikes of wheat twisted and practically tied around her strong head, slightly freckled white skin, and full forearms resembling two svelte vases with large flower-hands on top, this girl looked familiar, like he'd met her before, but where and when, he couldn't recall. And he didn't like her, even though he saw her as extraordinarily hard-working and silent, entirely dedicated to housework. Her very silence, enlivened by a faint gasp of physical well-being and the rigid fullness of her figure and even an animal scent that wafted around her, made her seem like a fine domesticated beast to him.

She would cook without once bending over the somewhat low stove and seemed to look down on the things she touched with a slight disdain. Every time the little girl attempted to approach, Ornella would forcefully push her back with the palm of her right hand. Ola returned, taking refuge with her grandfather, and both of them stayed next to the door, silent as well, as if they'd known each other for years and had already said everything.

The evening outside was still crisp, dark under the pergola, gray beyond, with a few glimmers of light coming from the tenant farmers' house. A scent of manure came from there as well, casting a pall over the garden's fragrance.

42

Once Ornella stopped frying, the murmur of the sea was heard, and against this cold, dull background noise, a cricket was already putting the metallic frills on his chirp.

But then, all of a sudden, like an unexpected gust of wind, something swept away the peace and quiet outside. The distinct crack of a whip was heard amidst a cluster of shrill notes from a bell, and then a youthful voice shouting *whoa, whoa* silenced all other sound. The little girl's eyes filled with light.

"It's Daddy," she said, standing on tiptoes as if to better see him in the distance. Then all atwitter, she drew near her grandfather and whispered in his ear:

"Shall we play a joke on him? Let's hide behind the door, and when he comes in, we can scare him!"

The grandfather agreed, and behind the door that Ola was pressing her mouth against to stifle her laughter, he was once again entirely under her spell.

But the dog that preceded his master threatened to spoil the practical joke when he darted inside, panting, tail in the air. Part happy and part suspicious, he quickly inspected the kitchen, galloping about like a little white horse with a black saddle and barking at the unfamiliar man. Realizing that Ola was motioning for him to be quiet, he stood hesitant, tail and head raised, watching the scene with his human eyes.

Even Ornella deigned to participate in the joke.

"Ola's not here. She went for a walk with her grandfather who arrived this morning," she said without turning when

Antonio entered. Accustomed to these tricks, he pretended to fall for it.

"Oh, great, they went off for a walk? And here I'd brought a little bird home for that rascal! I guess now I'll have to let it go."

She couldn't resist any longer. Pushing the door back, she shouted:

"Here we are! Here we are!"

And the two men embraced, intertwined with her, in silence.

7.

Words came later. First Antonio went to see his wife, and then asked Ornella to set the table. Finally, from the cellar he brought up two long bottles of wine so dusty they looked like they'd come from some archeological excavation of an ancient city, and he invited his father to the dinner table with a pat on the back as if to say:

"Finally! Finally I can pay you back something. Let's eat."

Even Tigrino, the stray cat with the blue-green eyes of an angel came back inside, and as he walked, he seemed to lengthen and contract from the coils of his gray, yellow, and brown stripes. And in an admirable pact with the dog, they both sat together under the table.

The table was set as if for the holidays. Ornella, guessing Antonio's intentions, had laid out the clean, ironed tablecloth, the plates without cracks, the crystal knife rests for the cutlery. Then she raised the lamp because light raining down from above softened everything.

And she seated Ola where she wouldn't disturb the two men, softly informing her that she would serve her, but she had to be quiet.

Ola did stay quiet, but clearly noticed the unusual pageantry and never took her eyes off her father because even he seemed different to her, better dressed than other days. That is, he looked finer and more handsome, but also vainer than usual. And she sensed the festive air, like when they would have guests, and despite being obliged to sit still and keep quiet, Ola would always enjoy herself more than anyone simply by listening to everything and seeing new faces. She was startled then when her father, after filling her grandfather's plate with white and red slices of ham like little flags, said with cheer and curiosity:

"Well now, tell me!"

And then even her grandfather took on a new guise. He was a man who had come from faraway lands and spoke to his son in a different way than he spoke to her. Even Ornella was different—oh, far different from the Ornella of those evenings when Momma was in bed. Now she had her white apron on and was serving the food with a bow like the waiters did in the little restaurant on the beach. An aura of fantasy surrounded the table, and she felt the way a theatergoer does when reality is turned upside down on stage, and yet touches the heart more than real life itself.

Grandfather spoke, interrupting his slow eating with his hollow, somewhat rocky voice. They weren't great adventures, but, well, they were things she didn't already know, had never heard, and her father's exclamations and interruptions, demonstrating that he was no less interested than she in the tales, further enlivened them.

Then he began to tell stories too, her father did. They were ones she knew, but when he told them, they sounded fresh, partly because he added details and emphasis that she hadn't yet heard. Once or twice she had the urge to set things straight, but didn't dare.

It was the teacher's turn to listen, and he looked at his son as if seeing him for the first time, and that sense of distance that he'd felt on his arrival, finding himself alone in front of the train station, returned to pierce his soul. The little girl's presence, however, once again bridged that desolate space.

"You've put on weight," he said, looking at the younger man's strong hands and powerful frame. "You've become a man."

He seemed to stress that final word, with a barely perceptible hint of regret, because it hadn't been him, as he had hoped, but life itself with its irresistible forces that had turned the boy into a man.

The young man heard it, and in part with sincerity and in part from the effect of the fine wine mixing with his blood, and not forgetting to look at himself from a distance the way a good actor does in the mirror on the wall in front of him, he began to recite.

"I owe it all to you! And I haven't forgotten a thing, no. The very state of well-being in which I currently find myself, I owe to your fine teaching, your example. At times when I found myself on the brink of the abyss, I immediately thought of you and felt myself pulled back. And that saintly woman lying in that bed of suffering can tell you how many times she's heard me pronounce your name in my sleep. And this beautiful creature can tell you how I speak of you ahead of God even—isn't that right, Ola?"

Ola burst out laughing—joyous laughter at seeing her father so solemnly addressing her. But that laughter might also have sounded like mockery, so Ornella gave her a little slap on the head as she cleared the table, without, however, showing that she had paid even the minimum attention to the two men's conversation.

"Let's not exaggerate," the schoolteacher said, with that slight hint of irony that echoed in his voice at times, unbeknownst to him. "I could have done more for you. The problem is that, like a real father, I was weak. But since fate has come to your aid and you're happy, let's thank the Lord. Happiness is with us."

He turned to the girl as well, giving her a nod. She was listening, her eyes radiant, and this time she didn't laugh because she hadn't really understood, but with a sweet movement of her head, she replied a bit ironically to her grandfather's nod.

And her father took another drink, lifting his glass to her.

8.

Once they were alone, the two men spoke more freely, smoking pipes. Even their pipes revealed their different nature: short and all one piece, made of briar wood blackened over time and with a prehistoric bowl for the teacher; long, with a silver-trimmed mouthpiece for Antonio. They even smoked differently: the elder man with tenacity and a profound voluptuousness, like a baby sucking his mother's breast; the younger with violence, pulling the pipe from his mouth every moment to spit mindlessly.

"Am I truly happy? Yes, I'm truly happy!" he exclaimed emphatically, but still sounded sincere. "I would be more so, certainly, if Marga, my wife, didn't have that affliction. Just between us—and it's the doctor's opinion as well—I believe it's a nervous condition more than anything else, one that I hope will pass with time and when she agrees to get away from here. But she's a stubborn woman as far as that goes—she never leaves the house and isn't fond of strangers."

"What about me then?"

"Oh, you're different. She's been waiting for you like the Messiah. She's been waiting for you for so long, and I think your presence is exactly what she needs."

"Yes, I noticed something strange in your wife's eyes and voice too. For example, she talks about her dead husband in an odd way."

Antonio brusquely laid his pipe on the table and laughed. But it was a false, theatrical laugh.

"There we are! That's precisely her obsession—remembering her famous Adelmo like some hero or saint. I think in part she does it to make me jealous. I never met this Adelmo, but I've heard plenty! He was a good bit older than her, and from a photograph that she keeps hidden away like a holy relic, you can see a long, ugly face that goes on and on, with two sunken harpy eyes. Moreover, they say that in his final years, during the war, he was quite partial to the enemy, communicating with them by means of his boats."

"You speak so ill of him, my son," the other man observed affably. "It seems your wife has indeed succeeded in making you jealous."

"No, no," protested Antonio, picking up his pipe and taking a long look at it as though he'd never seen it before. "That would be unnatural. And damn it, I'm healthy and happy, with no qualms and no concerns. In fact, this pipe—do you see it?—it belonged to the good Adelmo who bought it in Holland. I fully enjoy smoking with it."

In fact, he stuck it back in his mouth with an arrogant demeanor. Then the teacher thought that the pipe wasn't the only thing Antonio was availing himself of, and he didn't know why there was a taste like bad blood in his saliva.

Marga's veiled revelations all came to mind again.

"She's been waiting for me," he said, almost to himself. "She's a good woman, isn't she?"

"Good and capable. Incredibly hard working, totally devoted to the house, to me, to our little girl. You'll see that tomorrow. Besides, we're in total agreement on this: although it's her property, I put in all the work and all my blood to make it turn a profit. Today, for example, I should have come to meet you. No, sir, I had to run off to protect the family's interests. Indeed, I thought, 'He, my father, will be happy about it.'"

"You did the right thing, in fact."

"And everything's flourishing because that's how I am—in another's hands it all would have gone to ruin. And I account for every last cent to Marga. And for my part, as she could tell you herself, I live like I'm still under my parents' roof." Raising his voice and puffing out his chest, he continued: "Oh, but just because I ran away from home and hurt my benefactor, it doesn't mean I didn't become a gentleman."

The teacher felt like his innermost thoughts had been poked. He wasn't afraid of his own judgments, though, or of others guessing them. He actually enjoyed playing the part of a judgmental instructor when it was worthwhile, a habit perhaps left over from his school days when some pupil would secretly commit naughty deeds, and he would attempt to wrest the truth from his soul, enlightening the boy by simply revealing his wickedness.

Then he calmly said to Antonio:

"If Marga is trying to make you jealous, as you say, and lapses into this nervous manifestation of her illness, she must have some reason. A completely happy woman doesn't think of such things."

"What do we know of women? They all, more or less, have a streak of madness, especially when it comes to love. Marga was insanely jealous even with her first husband, who was old and far from a pinnacle of handsomeness. She would chase after him even at night, and she herself recounts the time that she followed him in a boat when he fished. Bad weather surprised them, putting her at risk of life and limb. With me though, she's never acted jealous, but I think she is, or at least she was, in the early days of our marriage."

"Marriage is a sacred thing," the teacher said solemnly, "and these clouds mustn't obscure it, especially when there are children. When a man marries, he assumes a responsibility before God. It's like a farmer who undertakes the cultivation of strong, healthy new plants from the seeds he will sow on the land entrusted to him. Children are the flower of life."

Antonio was smoking, almost vexed that his excellent qualities as a husband and father were being called into question.

"Marriage *is* a big responsibility," he finally said, reprising that declamatory tone that was like a veil over the sincerity of his words, "but if you had only taken a wife and knew how much prudence and patience it took to live in harmony, you wouldn't blame a man for sometimes looking outside the house for some innocent amusement."

"Oh, and there we are! You're laying the blame at your wife's feet, then."

"Blame, what blame? You can blame a man for stealing his wife's love, or worse, her possessions. But I can swear that I've never spent one red cent on a woman—they don't deserve it anyway. They're more or less all whores," he declared, spitting a long way, "and they're the ones who go around looking for men, especially ones who are—come on, to hell with modesty— young and strong like yours truly. Besides, exuberant health is precisely why a man needs some relaxation. Even good wives—like Marga, after all—don't pay much attention to it. We're not living in ancient times anymore, and for that matter, even Solomon needed more than one woman."

The teacher stopped smoking. He recognized that everything Antonio said was reasonable, but still felt displeasure and almost disgust.

"We're moving into the realm of vice, then," he replied, though with the sad certainty he wouldn't be understood, "and I admit to a certain negligence about love, but not about vice. A man must be satisfied with one woman, and a woman with one man. This is God's commandment as well as the law of nature. I do know that had I taken a wife, I would never have betrayed her."

"Which is precisely why you were so careful not to take one."

The teacher didn't immediately respond, but his face, which had been as pale and translucent as his glass, turned pink. Indignation, remorse, regret, maybe even pain, or maybe even shame? Maybe all together these hot-blooded flowers of passion had pummeled his soul.

"My dear son," he said, calling him that for the first time, "perhaps you're right. One can't judge what one doesn't know. And you and I, here, represent reality and dream in a way. You're alive, and I would be dead if death itself weren't life's great teacher. What do you know of me? How do you know that I'm not speaking precisely from experience, from having myself lived and sinned, and that my lessons aren't being given to you as a caution against future sorrow?"

But the other man only understood those words on the surface level.

"I know who I'm dealing with," he said, almost viciously. "I'm only too familiar with the world and the people in it to allow myself to be mistreated further. No one can hurt me."

"Pain doesn't come from others; it comes from ourselves and from nature. You're strong, yes, today, but tomorrow?"

"Tomorrow is in God's hands," the younger man replied cheerfully, pouring himself one last glass, shaking the empty, upside-down bottle as if trying to force it to release some wine hidden inside. But he didn't drink. Deep down, he was sorry that his father was so melancholy. Besides, he knew that a man who doesn't drink is always a bit preachy and tedious, and he wanted to shake him up, help him spend at least a few happy hours. He began by addressing him more as an equal and less as a father.

"I want to tell you how I met Marga, since we're talking about her."

First he went to see if Ornella had really retired to her humble little room adjoining the kitchen. Returning, he sat down and drank his last glass without realizing it.

"She's quite the busybody, that girl! She acts like she doesn't care about anything, but she's always got her ears pricked. Besides, it's her, Marga, who wants her in the house, only because she's jealous of servant girls, and because this one's related to her beloved Adelmo."

"Well then," he resumed with a soft, cheerful voice. "I was here, as you'll recall, a corporal with the customs department, preparing for the exam to become vice-brigadier. I had serious notions, ambitions—I was hoping to quickly advance to marshal, and with time reach the rank of general. Why not? With some effort I certainly could have done it. It was a period when I didn't think about women. I'd asked to be transferred to a city where I could study better, and also because the marshal's wife was here and she made us subordinates spend our free time working in her vegetable garden, which just happens to abut Marga's vineyard.

"Marga was a recent widow who stayed out of sight. I only knew her by name, or by reputation rather, because of all the gossip about her dead husband. They said he'd been a spy for the Austrians, that he'd unearthed a treasure, that he'd stolen

54

a nice wad of cash from an elderly aunt of his who had raised him, leading her to die of a broken heart. Working in the garden of the marshal's wife, I would look at Marga's vineyard, field, and house with a certain ironic curiosity, thinking about the widow who hadn't left her house for a year, grieving that fine fellow who had also, they said, enriched himself for her and left her everything.

"In the end, I thought that Adelmo must have profited tremendously by fishing during the war because his boats would go out even when it was prohibited. But people always find something to criticize when an individual makes money, and so they'd slander Adelmo the way they slander me now that I've married his widow. A lot of them say that I married her for profit, but I did it out of love for her.

"I loved her even before I met her, and it was, one might say, my first true love.

"I was still practically a boy, and even though I knew the world inside out and women didn't scare me, I'd never truly been head over heels in love.

"When the marshal's wife came down to the garden to oversee my work, she would always talk to me about her mysterious neighbor, telling me that she was very beautiful and had aroused great passion, even in one of Adelmo's brothers, who left for the island of Java due to his love for her, and who in fact lives there still, fortunately. She eventually told me that it wasn't even possible to see her because she received no one, save for her closest relatives, and would never set foot outside the house again, in devotion to the memory of her husband.

"'How much would you bet that I can somehow get to see her anyway?' I said to the marshal's wife one October day. 'It's not an ogre's house, after all, with no doors and no windows. And I'll find a way to see madam Marga in her room, in her very bedroom.'

"The marshal's wife was a beautiful woman as well, and mischievous, and she enjoyed my company. I think that's really why she made me work in the garden, to entertain herself by teasing me with incessant talk of love, women, and especially Marga.

"'Where there's a will, there's a way,' she said to me knowingly.

"'Whatever should happen, you'll be my witness that my intention was only to see this famous beauty up close.'

"I must confess that the marshal's wife was in cahoots with me in this enterprise, allowing me to open a gap in the hedge where I could enter the field here behind the garden. Like I said, it was October and the weather was still warm. In the barracks we were still sleeping with the windows open, and from mine I could see the glimmer from Marga's window through the pergola.

"Then one fine night I slipped into the field wearing felt shoes one uses to catch smugglers, and made my way, as quiet as a mouse. Oh, I forgot to tell you that I'd made friends with the tenant farmers' dog that would often approach the hedge and bark at our hens. I would toss him something to eat, and as you know, food is the best way to befriend a dog. He began to bark, in fact, as soon as I was in the field, but when he approached and recognized me, he quieted down. Then he even festively ran ahead, leading the way, as if he knew my intentions were good.

"And so I arrived next to the pergola. Marga's window—you've seen it—isn't very high above the ground. I got down on my knees, gradually approaching to see better. And fortune was on my side, perhaps too much so.

"Marga, who I believe was engaged in prayer for the soul of her dead husband, was washing her arms and neck, the way she still does before going to bed. And so I saw her with her shoulders and bosom bare, her hair pulled back, twisted on top of her head. She was as beautiful as a marble statue. When she dried off, vigorously rubbing her skin with the towel, she turned all pink. She stood and examined herself, turning her fresh, clean arms back and forth, then carefully inspecting a heart-shaped mole in the middle of her chest. I threw myself onto the ground, almost fearfully. And I stayed there until she closed the shutters and everything was silent.

"And I didn't say a word to the marshal's wife, preferring to lose the bet, just so I could continue the game in peace. Then one night, Marga's tenant farmer noticed me and came within a hair's breadth of shooting me. I said I was within my rights to enter whenever I pleased for official business. And since I was madly in love and wanted to talk to Marga so bad I couldn't stand it anymore, I added that I in fact had to search her house. Complete turmoil ensued. Marga, who lived alone with a servant girl, panicked such that I felt guilty for having disturbed her. The farmer's wife and mother came running, disheveled like two witches. The dog lost all sense of restraint and began barking, but as if protesting all that pointless activity.

"'Madam,' I said to Marga, 'I've been ordered to inspect your terrace because it seems that, unbeknownst to you, someone has managed to deposit contraband merchandise there.'

"She didn't protest, didn't offer any resistance. She had them give me the key to the terrace and ordered the farmer to accompany me. I said her presence was necessary, and she came with us. Naturally, there was nothing to find. I did notice though that a little door from the attic opened onto the terrace, and requested that Marga open it. She sent the man down to get the key. Once alone, I knelt before her and asked her forgiveness.

"'You are the only contraband I was looking for. I dreamed up this method of seeing you because there was no other way.'

"At first she jumped back, frightened, and then she laughed out loud and said in dialect: 'What a stupid imbecile you are!'

"And yet, when I came back to call on her in broad daylight, not only did she welcome me, but she sent the servant girl away on an errand so we could be alone to talk at our leisure."

9.

Marga got up at dawn the next day, and it was like the sun bursting out in a house that had been overcast without her.

When the teacher, all neat and combed, entered the kitchen, she had already tidied up the rooms, visited the tenant farmers, talked to the cows, the little colt, the mare, the hens and the ducks, the water in the well, and the plants and flowers.

Now she was talking to the kitchen utensils. Everything was fair game to receive her expressions of joy at being alive and moving about.

Except Ornella, the teacher noted, to whom she constantly directed criticism, and who received it in silence, impassive as a statue. Marga immediately calmed down, however, resuming her laughter and addressing little Ola like a grown-up and finally turning to him, her father-in-law, calling him as a witness to the advantages that she enjoyed in life.

"Do you see? Antonio has already left, without having so much as a sip of water. He's gone to take care of our business, while another man would stay snug in bed like a lord and master. Everything goes well at home when one gets up early and does one's duty."

Then, as she was pouring coffee and milk into cups and cutting pieces of leftover bread from the night before on a tray, she asked the girl:

"Did you say your prayers? Did you pray for your wonderful father too? — You'll see, Grandfather, that this little girl will be a true woman, content with herself and others. She'll even study Latin, God willing, without neglecting the domestic virtues. The example of her parents, and now you as well, will be a big help to her. And how beautiful this girl is, and how kind! There's none other like her in the world. — What are you doing, Ola, you ugly, wicked little thing? You're my cross to bear on this earth!"

Had the teacher not been there, she would have slapped her, since Ola, making the most of that maternal praise, had bent over and was pouring some of her milk with coffee on the dog's back. The dog had stayed home since his master didn't need to go any farther than the port where they unloaded fish, but it seemed he'd stayed simply to become better acquainted with the guest, and was running around him, sniffing to carefully study him and to let the man get to know him better. For his part, the teacher allowed himself to be moved by that affection-craved creature's almost human panting, tossing bits of bread that the animal caught in mid-air with his red tongue, the black spot on his back glistening like velvet and his whole spine quivering with joy and gratitude.

The cat, on the other hand, refused to approach. He loved robust, refined foods, and now, stretched out on a chair, paws and tail tucked in, motionless like a little tiger-striped marble sphinx, he awaited Ornella's return from grocery shopping.

The schoolteacher truly loved these domestic portraits. He sensed something of a Biblical air in them and breathed easier.

Marga's overwrought figure—with her shabby, faded dress, which didn't however hide the natural elegance of her fine, supple body, and her hair in disarray around her silvery, highly mercurial face—drew a stark contrast to her innocent surroundings, and he felt that her joy was a bit like her words: an iridescent veil that she shook in front of others to fool them and herself.

Marga became a bit nervous when Ornella returned from shopping and the table was loaded with paper bags and vegetables still damp from the garden, and some cups got knocked over, and the cat jumped up in a determined search for meat. She pushed away Ola, who was also rummaging through the packages, spilling the rice and flour, and then began scolding Ornella again.

The teacher's suggestion to go for a walk—he, the girl, and the dog—was welcomed with gratitude by all.

And so they went, those three, small and alone in the vastness of the beach and the blue of the sea.

The stretch of naked sand, still untainted by human footprints, was preceded by grass-covered fields and little yellow and purple flowers seemingly made of crystal. Everything was crystal-clear and gemstone-colored: the sky, the water, the seashells, and the sand itself there where the waves retreated and the sun refracted as if through a prism. But what especially attracted the teacher's and Ola's gaze was a

61

large, blazing triangle stretched out on the green grass. It was a canvas sail that an old seafaring artist had painted a saffron color and was now working on with scrupulous technique, drawing paint from buckets set out around him, stepping back a bit from time to time to better observe the painting's effect.

At the top was the sun, red, with long, scattered rays like when it rises over the sea. Below that, a yellow streak separated the upper part of the sail from the lower, and although everything was brightly colored, one had the impression that a neutral zone, like that of sand, divided the landscape, majestic in its linear simplicity. And so, there was the infinite on top, the sun's immense radiance, and below, where the saffron died down to a beige, the earth lived in that light.

On the golden patch, the artist finished painting a rooster with a shade of pomegranate. Even that symbolized the idea of a new day, jubilant with hope and love.

The teacher felt a superstitious joy in his heart, since by now everything held a symbolic, fairy tale-like quality for him.

10.

He and his two companions stood there watching for a good while. Even Birba the dog, although apparently slow to comprehend the significance of the canvas, ran around it, innocently barking at the rooster as if worried it would spring out alive from the tip of the paintbrush, and at the paintbrush itself, until the arrival of another little dog distracted him.

They ran to each other, circling about and sniffing before reciprocally jumping on one another and rolling around on that grassy carpet, biting in a gentle, playful battle, happy as little children who were longtime friends.

"Men, on the other hand," said the teacher, trying to start a conversation with the painter, "when they meet for the first time, they regard each other as enemies."

The painter in fact raised his turquoise eyes with indifference, irritated by the stranger's insistent curiosity, and pushed back the girl who was getting too close to the canvas. Then she tried to join in on the dogs' play, but her grandfather led her away, a bit roughly. Even Birba, despite repeated calls, wouldn't abandon his new friend, who finally decided to follow him.

The beach was completely deserted. Ola tried pulling her grandfather to the left, towards the palisade of the pier that looked like a bridge between land and sea, with the black figures of people on it, stamped against a deep blue background, but he was attracted by the great silence and vast solitude to the right, where the line of sand evaporated into the blue and seemed to disappear into the far-off mountain on the horizon.

"Is that your town down there?" Ola asked, and he nearly jumped, squeezing that sweet, warm little hand in his because she'd delved directly into his thoughts.

"No, that's not my town—mine is further down, but I'm thinking about it right now."

"Is the sea there, at your town?"

"Oh, no. There are mountains that are… See, like these trenches that the soldiers made with sand, but much, much bigger, tall, covered with trees and shrubs."

"Is the Mammon Cat there?" she asked, a bit terrified by the magnitude of all that unknown.

"No, no, sweetheart. The Mammon Cat doesn't exist."

She protested. No, she wouldn't let her heritage of intense feelings be stolen. She stopped and dug her heels in.

"No, the Mammon Cat really does exist, you know! I heard it myself, at night, when all the doors and windows were shut: *Meow! Meow!*"

And she even bit her grandfather's hand a little to enhance her impersonation.

"Okay, okay," he said, pretending to be scared and letting go of her little hand to blow on his own. "Go away, Mammon Cat!"

Once again, her laugh seemed more iridescent than the sea and the flowering fields, and almost afraid of that moment of joy, he turned away so she wouldn't see that he was laughing too.

"Let's play some more," she suggested, taking his hand again.

They played like the two dogs on the beach, like the minnows in the sea, like the little lilac-colored butterflies skimming the waves.

Until Ola got carried away and really bit his hand, and he sternly stood up.

"A good game doesn't last long, and when it does, it becomes a nuisance."

Then they went to see the trawlers return from fishing. They came back two by two, like married couples after a nice walk. As they reached the shore, re-entering the channel with a dignified unhurriedness, one of the fishermen would climb up on the boat's bulwarks like a monkey, and from there would grab onto the edge of the wharf and jump onto it. A mate would toss him the dock line which he would then tie to the iron rings lodged between the stones of the wharf. Once tied up like a big, placid, winged beast, the boat would rock quite a bit before settling motionless on the water that so clearly reflected it.

One after another they all lined up along the wharf, sails blazing in the air and painted hulls in the water, some seemingly tattooed by the many patches cutting into their designs. And all around, a festive atmosphere reigned, as if a parade were passing by, with sparkling golden and silver banners.

Ola in fact pointed out to her grandfather the metal decorations and the carvings on some of the new boats: deep blue stripes, silvery plates, and even vases of flowers stood out against the pitch-black wood. But what she liked the most was an all-gold griffin with red eyes that stuck out from a bow and glistened like an idol in the sun. She showed him her father's boats as well, but wasn't very proud of them. There were four of them, rather small and old, although fully renovated, with a coat of white varnish. And if they had had white sails, they would've looked like two pairs of doves, the way they were huddled together, touching, kissing each other. Their names, however—*San Giorgio* and *Nicoletta*, *Gabbiano* and *Maria Margherita*—didn't match, except for the dark blue color of the big letters, all decorated with flourishes.

But their sails were simple, all a bright shade of saffron yellow, brand new, denoting their new owner's ardent, intrepid nature.

Onboard, like on the other boats, silent, shoeless fishermen, with their broad, webbed feet damp with seawater and skin burnt by salinity, sorted fish with amazing rapidity. In a few moments the black baskets were filled to the brim with large, oily gray sole fish, silvery mullets, and plump, flesh-pink mullets. Red crayfish, still waving their serrated claws, were tossed aside with disdain, along with piles of rejected minnows, naked and slippery as worms.

Then the baskets were loaded onto wheelbarrows, pushed by fishermen who seemingly sprung from the sea after gathering up the fish there, the way farmers harvest the fruits of the earth.

Ola, her grandfather, and the dog followed them. Here and there on the glistening rocks of the wharf lay dead minnows, spilled from the baskets. The teacher tried to avoid stepping on them out of a sense of pity that the big fish from the catch hadn't aroused in him, and Ola, as if reading his mind once again, bent over and with two tiny fingers picked those little fish up and tossed them into the sea. The water opened and closed like a small mouth to swallow them up.

"Will they come back to life, Grandfather? No, right? When they're dead, they don't ever come back to life."

His heart skipped a beat because suddenly an ominous memory passed through the broad light of his immense happiness.

Meanwhile, he unwittingly let Ola lead him along, and Ola followed the fishermen, full of self-confidence. She knew them all, and they all knew her. She even knew the names of the dogs and cats from the boats and greeted them all with faint smiles and nods.

Then she compelled her grandfather to stop and watch a fisherman with his line, knowing it would provide an interesting show. The man, decently dressed, sat on the edge of the wharf, holding a rod from which a line dangled, sinking into the water. Motionless, head bowed, he seemed to be praying "Lord God, send me a nice big fish that I can take home to fry and feed my family, amen."

Other children looked on silently, and everyone's expression seemed one of expectation for a big event.

Even the grandfather became curious, as if caught up in the general anxiety, and he wondered if such a pastime might be good for himself as well.

A wave rippled around the line as it sunk deeper, of its own accord, into the water. The man immediately raised the rod and the children's mouths opened as if to ingest the already well-cooked fish. Then a smile of disappointment mixed with mockery for the fisherman crossed everyone's face because swinging there at the end of the line, stuck on the hook, shiny as a dangling earring, was just the sad, dead, little fish used for bait.

Not sharing in the general anxiety, the fisherman remained undaunted. Unaccustomed to others participating in his fishing, he didn't let his disappointment or his renewed hope show.

Slowly he lowered the bait back into the water's gentle depths and hunched forward to wait once more.

"Ola, let's go," said the grandfather, squeezing and jerking the little girl's hand, but she had her good reasons not to move and begged him to wait.

Then the fisherman pulled the rod back with surprising deftness, and before the bystanders realized what was happening, a fine, nearly blue fish was desperately flopping around in the basket, tangled in the line.

And now the man pushed the children back who were hollering with joy as if the fish belonged to them, and he smiled with both irony and satisfaction.

"He who laughs last, laughs best."

But he quit laughing when the grandfather, after leaning over to hear Ola whisper a suggestion in his ear, asked him if the fish was for sale.

Of course it was for sale—the fisherman hoped to catch more to take home. They haggled as the victim in the basket continued its glittering, hopeless dance, and its large eyes ringed in coral red grew dim like a drowned man's. Then its bounces gradually grew slower and shorter. Its twisted body stretched out, dropping to the bottom of the basket where it came to rest diagonally. Finally, after one final wriggle, it fell again and lay inert, with its stomach growing pale and its fins folding up like little fans.

"It's dead," the children announced. The fisherman wrapped it in a funeral shroud of newspaper and handed it to the buyer. And so they left, the grandfather and the little girl, along the sun-drenched pier. The dog followed, having witnessed the entire scene with little interest, though, because he didn't like fish in any way, shape, or form.

The palisade of the pier ended in the street that skirted the canal, which in turn suddenly broadened into an open space surrounded by trees and cluttered with lumber. It was both the seamen's worksite and the fish market.

Ola dragged her grandfather that direction and then suddenly pulled her hand free from his to run toward a group of men and women standing in front of baskets of fish. Her father was among them, his hat high on his head and his tie, as dazzling as a summer butterfly, in fine display on his blue shirt. She hugged his legs, laughing.

He turned. Seeing the teacher, he waved, but seemed annoyed by his presence. Perhaps he didn't feel it was the proper moment to introduce him to his acquaintances. Besides, they didn't show the slightest interest in the stranger, who likewise had no desire to make friends with anyone. He was happy with the companionship he'd already found, and when Ola, gently shooed away by her father, returned to him, he took hold of her little hand again like something that belonged exclusively to him, determined to never let her run off again.

And so, as if trying to stay hidden to avoid bothering Antonio, they moved a short distance away to watch the fish market. It was carried out in a unique way, one colored with mystery, which explained the almost tragic attention, the harsh faces, and the eyes filled with selfishness of those involved.

The auction began with a fine basket of mullets, so blazingly red it seemed to be filled with fresh-cut flowers. The main figure of the picturesque group, a big, tall man in a loose-fitting black jacket which jutted out in all directions, shouted some words in dialect, inviting buyers to place their bids. Then one by one, men and women approached, and standing on tiptoe since he would lean neither to the right nor to the left, whispered into his ear the amount they intended to offer.

He listened impassively, his jovial face bathed in sunlight. He must not have been satisfied, though, because he repeated his call and again received secret bids, appearing to take confession from all those somber people caught up in a competition upon which their fate seemed to hang.

The basket of mullets was finally awarded to a large, disheveled woman who reeked of fish gone bad, the only one who could easily speak into the auctioneer's ear and who seemed his rival. She made her way through the crowd with palms as oily as fish, smiled at the mullets as she lifted the basket and placed it in her wheelbarrow, and then took off, ignoring everything else.

Ola squeezed her grandfather's hand and they left too, in the wake of that marine odor left behind by the stout fishwife, and they walked the entire length of the street along the canal. Beyond that strip colored by the boats' sails and their reflections in the green water, a bright, gray cloud of desolate tamarisks rose up, and in the distance, pine trees made the sky seem bluer still. Then the street turned, plunging sharp, direct, and shiny like a sword into the heart of the town.

And this heart was a small piazza paved with pebbles from the beach, a church standing on the right, the old black city hall building on the left, a dry fountain in the middle, and above, a symmetrical block of sky like a deep blue ceiling, everything pulsating with the sound of bells and the buzzing of the crowd in the central marketplace.

The well-stocked windows of the fabric and food stores made it feel like being in a city. So much so that the grandfather would have felt a bit lost had Ola not confidently led the way.

First she drew him to the closest corner of the piazza, in front of her favorite shop window, crammed with valuable and interesting items like a museum: dressed-up dolls, winged and naked good-luck cherubs, lacquered bracelets and baubles. He played dumb, though, since a cornerstone of his former

71

profession was to avoid nurturing children's love for useless things.

"The doll that I brought you," he said to console her, "is a thousand times prettier than these, and it's a good-luck charm to boot." And then for greater consolation, he stopped in front of another shop window. "At least they have useful things here. Oh, look at the beautiful tarts with a cherry ruby in the center! Look at the nice little cookies still as warm as your tiny fingers! Look at the lovely cream pastries that seem to be parting their lips to show off their filling and say *eat us, eat us, eat us*. Should we take some home to your mom?"

The pastry shop was filled with the scent of sugar as they entered, and the first little tart atop the dignified pyramid on the tray at the counter was plucked like a beautiful tea rose from the top of a bush and offered to Ola. She accepted it, not greedily, but hastily, and turned it round and round to look at it. She ran her finger all around it, then her tongue, searching for the best spot to attack, and once it was found, she sunk her teeth in with a ruthless movement, but then gradually eased her assault until arriving at the last little bite, which she pulled from her mouth and looked at all over again, breaking it into bits which she ended up eating crumb by crumb. The last one fell to the floor, and she picked it up.

"And that's how life is," the teacher thought, watching her while the confectioner, with a melancholy and disgusted expression, arranged sweets on a cardboard tray for them to take home.

11.

Ola, though, followed the affair with great interest, and when the pretty white package was ready, neatly fastened with a tricolor ribbon and a loop for sticking your finger in to carry it, she tugged on the hem of her grandfather's jacket and made him listen to one of her secrets.

"Give me another one."

But he wanted to mold her, and so despite a heavy heart, he didn't give in.

"When we get home."

To further console her, he let her carry the package, and they stepped back out into the crowded piazza, which felt like a large, shared courtyard. Everyone knew each other there, and even Ola was giving and receiving smiles left and right, while the women selling fruit and vegetables focused their curious attention on the man accompanying her.

"Is that your grandfather?"

"Yes, he's my grandfather," she would reply, tugging his hand, proud of him, even though his apprehension prevented her from accepting apples or peas the women would offer. She responded to one woman haughtily however, pulling back. She wasn't a merchant, though, just some ordinary old woman, hunched over a fat cane, with large feet that looked dead and a big black scarf tied around her small face the color and shape of a wrinkly pear.

"God bless you," she said, despite Ola's rude response. Thinking her a beggar, the teacher offered a coin which she refused with no sign of indignation, shaking her tremulous head as if to say: "Money is good, but it takes more than that to get along." Saying nothing more, she went on her way with the slow, silent gait of a tortoise.

"Who's that?" the teacher asked.

"She's the old woman from the Ontani house. She steals children."

"I find that hard to believe. Where is this house?"

"I'll show you. Momma doesn't want me going up there. But with you, I can, right?"

And she gave him a mighty tug, already bewitched by the thought of forbidden fruit. As they passed the steps of the old church occupying one entire side of the piazza, the teacher thought he'd like to go in, to see where Ola had been baptized and where she might one day be married. He himself didn't practice any organized religion, having his own particular one, the certainty that God resides within us and that we reside within God, and we can find answers in the sound of *our own* voices. But he was convinced that Christianity was the sole starting point for unsophisticated souls to arrive at that level of perfect awareness.

So he placed his foot on the first step, heading up to the door of the church. Ola, however, pulled him back and was about to say, "What are you doing? Are you crazy?" But already familiar with the lights and shadows of his face, she astutely said, "We'll go in tomorrow, you'll see. Tomorrow's Sunday. Momma is waiting for us now."

Despite that stated concern, she took the long way home. She led her grandfather back along the boulevard from the station all the way to the path that led to their house, but instead of heading that direction, she made him go the opposite way.

There the path broadened out into a nice road, between the sandy shore and the little gardens of some small houses hidden behind tamarisk shrubs. Towards the beach, the trenches made during the war appeared again, little grass-covered hills, some so high they blocked the view of the sea. After that, the road rose, all trace of human habitation disappeared, and a line of very dense alder trees blocked the right horizon.

Ola had given the package back to her grandfather, and now it was she holding his hand tight, and every now and then she would look back with a slightly calculated but also sincere fear. That was how they arrived in front of an iron gate cloaked in a metallic lattice, blocking the typical pathway that led to a modest, grayish, two-story house surrounded by trees. The place looked deserted.

"This is where the old woman lives," said Ola, jerking her grandfather's hand since he didn't seem particularly smitten by the mystery of the spot.

The house didn't actually look at all special. It resembled so many others one could see a bit off the beaten track in agricultural towns along the seashore, accompanied by a vineyard under the watchful eye of a farmers' hut, and behind that, a tilled field of beets completed the picture.

But the thing that captured Ola's attention and ended up intriguing her grandfather as well was a grassy clearing to the right of the house, where the shadows of tall trees quivered as if in dense green water. Amidst these shadows, the lonely whiteness of a few marble benches and two large, round tables, also marble, whose crisp starkness, adorned by fallen leaves from the trees, conveyed to the grandfather the sense of solitude and sadness that must have loomed over that abandoned house. Ola, a bit hesitantly, explained the mystery to him.

"The house is cursed, you know. The sons killed their father and ran away. But they caught one and sent him to prison, and the house belongs to the soldiers now. But the soldiers don't stay there. A man from another town lives there, along with that old woman who steals children."

"What about the mother?"

"What mother? The old woman's?"

"No, the mother of the evil sons."

"She's dead. Don't you know she's *dead*!" she exclaimed forcefully as if to say: *If the mother were alive, the crime never would have happened.*

"Was it a long time ago?"

"That she died?" asked the girl who adored precise speech.

"No, that the crime occurred."

Ola raised her hand and pursed her lips.

"Who knows! I don't know. Maybe it's been a hundred years. Maybe two years," she added, uncertain. When it came to time, precision abandoned her.

"You're right. In these cases, time doesn't matter. Come, come," he said, pulling her back from the gate. They went to sit on the side of the road, amidst the grass and flowers, in view of the sea. Ola would have liked to play a bit, racing after the saffron-colored butterflies that had a predilection for approaching her, seemingly to invite her to follow them, but she was afraid of the old woman and kept looking over her shoulder to see if she was coming. She also persisted in recounting the details of the patricide, not without a morbid streak, until her grandfather changed the subject.

"Tell me something, Ola, has Ornella been at your house a long time?"

"Oh, ever since that day she came!"

"Does she love you?"

"Sure she loves me, but she hits me sometimes. But I'm naughty, too. I put potatoes and pins in her bed."

"Why?"

"Because," she said with a grimace that meant: *Just for the fun of being mean.*

"You mustn't be wicked to anyone," he began in a lecturing tone, but the sound of his voice brought back that sense of anxiety he'd felt on the bridge of the pier.

Then they very slowly made their way back home.

Sometimes Ola would escape his grasp and, despite his protests, climb up on the embankments along the lane, threatening to stay unless he came up to get her. When that pleasure was denied her, she'd rush down headlong and crash into him like she wanted to knock him over.

"You're beginning to take too many liberties, and you're ill-mannered as well. But I'll see to setting you straight. I will indeed."

The grandfather was truly indignant, and she lowered her head and walked, mortified. He was moved by the sight of her legs: half bare, straight, identical, smooth like pink marble. Those were the columns upon which his entire world rested now. The shadows of a moment ago were followed by a great light, and he recalled a religious song that they'd taught him in a time long ago, one that he remembered only two partial verses of:

> *The sailor on the waves*
> *Invokes you, oh Lord…*

Nothing else. But the same way that scattered ruins offer a glimpse of a metropolis lost in the sands of time, an entire majestic symphony of hope and love rose up from those few words of that far-off hymn.

"I am grateful, Lord, and beg your forgiveness for still doubting that I've found my haven. Here I am, in the sun, with this little one, with Thee. I've sinned, and perhaps haven't yet atoned, but my heart will be pure as well as my flesh until the moment of my death. And I offer it all to you, and you can even visit me with all manner of pain and suffering, just so long as evil never touches the young life now walking beside me."

He took Ola's little hand again, and they walked in silence.

When they approached the house, their happiness was again upset by the sound of Ola's mother scolding Ornella. That harsh voice fell silent, though, when the dog, always running ahead of them, announced their approach. Even the cat greeted them at the door with an arched back, and the teacher, who really loved cats, took heart. This one had an overbearing but handsome face with two almost blue eyes that especially stood out against its velvety gold and brown fur.

Bending over to pet him, the teacher felt him slip out of his hand like a live eel, but he predicted that they would soon become friends.

Another nice surprise awaited them. On the white board for kneading flour, several regiments of an army of pale *agnolotti* pasta stretched out, and from the oven came the aroma of a sauce that triumphed over the garden's scent.

Marga was running around the kitchen, constantly bending and lifting, always carrying something. Still disheveled and with her clothes in disarray, she looked like she'd just had a dustup with someone, and when she saw the pastry package and the wrapped fish that the teacher set on the table, she became rather annoyed, not for the trouble he'd gone to, but because the new purchases upset the balance of the kitchen again. Nevertheless, she thanked him warmly and took it out on Ola.

"You shouldn't have allowed Grandfather to go to all that trouble. Or maybe it was you who took him to the fish market and the piazza. I know you, you little scamp, I know you. And now I have to cook the fish. Get this paper out of here. Get this package out of here. Did you at least thank him? No, I didn't think so. Thank him now."

Perhaps in an attempt at emulation, the girl had adopted Ornella's infallible method: she never responded directly to those maternal rebukes. Instead, she would change the subject to change her mother's mood.

"Yes, Momma, we went to the fish market and saw Daddy. And Gina Bluvin was there, in a dress with yellow stripes like Tigrino…"

Details that the grandfather had completely forgotten reappeared in her account. She lined up everything she'd collected and brought home on the edge of the table, like the little shells she pulled from her pocket. Her grandfather didn't even know where she'd found them.

Her mother listened childishly.

12.

Two weeks passed that way, happy and animated in the mother's days of good health, with long meals that left those at the table in a daze, especially in the evenings when the bottles arrived one after another, dusty and seemingly still frozen from the chilly darkness of the cellar, and Marga and Antonio would compete, inviting and encouraging each other to do the honors, and some old friend of the family would come to bolster the couple's goodwill.

After drinking, Marga would strangely settle down, sitting at the table silent, only occasionally adjusting her hair from force of habit. Her eyes, filled with a dreamy languor, and her fine face, illuminated as if in the glimmer of sunset, took on great beauty, seemingly the very picture of happiness. Antonio, on the other hand, usually busy, taciturn, and almost surly during the day, would become effusive and boastful. According to him, everything in the world was going well for him and was only bound to improve in the future.

"With this head and this heart, and having to work for this little one here, everything is bound to go well, by God!"

A fist to his forehead and chest, a hand theatrically extended towards Ola, and his fluctuating tone—energetic, tender, menacing—imbued his words with power. And Ola's laughter and her eyes gleaming with joy and mischief illuminated the table around which the schoolteacher, despite the happy appearances, persisted in seeing an aura of darkness.

Calmer, though shrouded in melancholy, were the days of Marga's fever. She seemed to collapse mainly from the excessive exertion and commotion of her healthy days, the way someone drops into deep sleep after prolonged wakefulness. On those days the teacher made it his duty and habit to not abandon the house and the girl. He taught her to read and write, discovering that the task of being a teacher had never seemed more difficult.

Ola resorted to every trick in the book to escape her obligation. When it was time for her lesson, she became deaf and mute and made him search for her a long time before deciding to jump out of her hiding places. Then she always had some illness before her lesson—her stomach ached, or her foot, or even the hand that was supposed to hold the pen.

And when she had somehow or other learned to write the letter *O*, she drew two little eyes and a crooked mouth in it, added two tiny feet underneath, and showed it to Ornella as a portrait of her grandfather.

"Oh, come on!" he lamented. "When it comes to your studies, you're as much of a blockhead as your father."

So she took a small block of wood and put it under his pillow, and when he complained, she replied: "It's a piece of my head."

13.

On the days when Antonio was away and Marga in bed, a profound silence, barely pierced by Ola's trills, reigned in the house warmed and brightened by the late spring. From the sea and the reed- and crocus flower-covered meadows along the beach, came a healthy fragrance that gave the teacher an almost physical sense of joy. He felt rejuvenated.

Even his little bedroom seemed transformed. By himself he had covered the walls with bright paper, golden as if sundrenched. Some small paintings and two rugs, inexpensive, but brightly colored, lent a distinguished air.

There was never a lack of flowers, mainly wild ones, in a rustic tankard converted to a vase.

Now while he was reading or writing, Ola would stretch out on one or the other rug, concentrating on deciphering its designs, tracing them with her fingertip and mumbling to herself. The cat would get in the way and reach his paw out towards her finger, playfully trying to scratch her. The dog was allowed in too, provided he didn't get too settled in. Even the chickens stuck their necks through the doorway, looking in with just one eye.

Another visitor greeted with ambiguous signs ranging from fondness to hostility was Lenin, a pink piglet with an upturned curlicue tail and lively eyes that sank into his fat more with each passing day. He would just barge right in, sniffing the floor and diving under the bed, where he took the liberty of emitting certain unpleasant-smelling sounds until the dog, after looking at the teacher's face as if to determine his feelings on the matter, drove the pig away and then kept chasing him even outside the room to punish him for his nasty impertinence.

The least welcome face was that of Ornella. The teacher avoided her, even when she cleaned his room. Not that the young woman didn't demonstrate the deepest respect to him, but her presence unsettled him—a physical unease that wasn't desire, but rather repugnance. She seemed obtuse to him, incapable of any instinct beyond a bestial one. And in recent days, he'd discovered her to be a liar and a fraud. Marga, for example, would order her to purchase goods from certain vendors, but Ornella instead went to others who gave her shoddy merchandise at a higher price. One day the teacher, at the behest of his daughter-in-law, went to complain at one of the vendors, who took it poorly and ended up insulting him.

"Marga," he said then, kindly but firmly, "don't send me on any more errands like that. Instead, I'll do the shopping myself. And please don't raise your voice with Ornella on my account over this."

Marga didn't raise her voice. She only asked her husband to order the young woman never to set foot in the insolent vendor's shop again, and Antonio did so with an exaggerated earnestness that seemed to make an unusual impression on Ornella.

That same day, however, the teacher happened to see her returning to buy from the forbidden shop. Then later, while he and Ola were behind the garden hedge, they heard her returning home with another young woman, and she seemed a different person the way she talked and laughed indecently, filled with all the liveliness of a beast in the springtime.

"That's how she always is, when Momma and Daddy aren't around," the girl said, noticing her grandfather's antagonistic surprise.

That's when a conspiracy was born between them. Without being asked, Ola would report to him every bad thing she caught Ornella doing, exaggerating them to make them sound worse, while always begging her grandfather not to say a word to anyone.

He noticed, however, that when she was alone with the young woman and didn't think anyone was looking, she would show a strange attachment to her. One day he saw them playing like cats, biting and roughing up one another.

He mentioned it to Marga, when Ornella went out.

Her face red with an immediate rage, the woman called the girl and began scolding her bitterly, as if she alone were responsible, and she would have hit her, absent the grandfather's intervention.

"No, not like that, not like that," he said, filled with anguish, hugging the girl tight, feeling himself seemingly take refuge in her as Marga went pale and her eyes clouded over with sorrow. All three fell silent as if surprised by a whirlwind trying to sweep them away, but what horrified them most was the mystery of her depraved violence.

With the drowsy voice of her feverish days, Marga began to apologize.

"What do you expect? Ignorant people are all like that, like that young woman, a bit animalistic. They're ignorant and deserve pity because they're unfortunate too. Ornella is far from the worst, and she loves the girl. Maybe she loves her in her own way, but she does love her. Isn't that right, Ola? When you were little," she added, apologizing to her too, "do you remember that cursed Tonina? She'd hit you if she heard you crying and drink the milk meant for your din-din. Ornella,

85

on the other hand, would run through the woods at night to summon a doctor if you didn't feel well and needed one."

"And besides, she sneaks me candies," Ola corroborated.

"But you mustn't cross the line with her, do you understand? Don't be foolish with her. If you only knew," she continued, addressing the teacher, "how many housekeepers I tried, each worse than the last. Ornella, at least, is dependable. She'll get up at night if she thinks she hears a suspicious noise and is capable of facing down thieves on her own."

Words upon words. They dropped into the void and expanded its darkness. And the woman felt it.

"I know," she resumed, more animated, "I should speak with Ornella and set her straight myself. But it's like talking to a wall—she doesn't understand a thing. Do animals understand?" she asked, looking at the teacher as though they'd agreed to speak to each other in a language the girl couldn't comprehend. "Besides, I can't and won't demean myself to her. I often scold her, that's true, for trivial things, and she enjoys what she knows is simply a game. But if I were to try saying even one single word truly attacking her, she's capable of lunging for my neck and strangling me."

The teacher felt an internal shudder because he was certain of Ornella's hidden violence—a single glance at her feline eyes was all it took.

"Then send her away," he said softly.

With the same tone, the woman responded: "If she were simply a servant, I could. But we have a moral responsibility to her as well. It would be like throwing her out into the street, because she has nowhere to go. Unless, of course, she took a position with someone else, and we don't want that. Besides," she added in a heartfelt voice, "she or another, it's all the same."

"Wouldn't an older woman be suitable?" the master suggested.

But Marga's hopeless resignation knew no bounds. "It's all the same. It's all the same. Inside or outside, it's all the same."

Those last words, pronounced with the same tone as in her delirium, cast a noose around the teacher's neck. He felt like he was suffocating.

"Ola," he said to the girl who was poking him in the back and no longer involved in her mother's tragic conversation. "You're annoying me. I'm not the cat, you know. Go on, go back outside and play. — Go on!" he ordered when she hesitated.

"Marga," he said when they were alone. "You realize that you should think of me as a father. Do you think that your husband and Ornella…?"

When Marga's eyes suddenly widened and closed again, like a door that opens before being immediately slammed shut as danger threatens, he almost felt ashamed of his assumption. But then her smile, also quick, revealing and then immediately hiding her oddly young, avid teeth in that wrinkled, worn-out face, weighed heavy on his heart because he sensed that Ola's worst enemy in that circle of mystery was her very own mother. Almost harshly he asked:

"You don't think that Antonio and Ornella could possibly have an illicit relationship?"

"Antonio is young, but if he needs to have fun, he does it out of the house," she replied, furrowing her brow.

"Inside or out, you shouldn't allow it, for your daughter's sake," he concluded harshly.

And since she laughed, seemingly mocking his naiveté, he went outside, took Ola by the hand, and led her to the beach to breathe in that immense air that cures every ill.

"Oh, sea," he thought as Ola dug in the sand with her tenacious little hands, "I feel like you're truly earth's soul and that you're there to teach us the nature of our own souls. The earth renews slowly with its seasons, like our bodies, but you renew every single moment in your bottomless abysses with the monsters and divine wonders of your infinite depths, like our souls."

And it felt like he'd finally found a true friend, a counterpart, one he could confide in better than any human being because they truly understood each other.

The sea was calm now, with an emerald ring in the distance and a wake of sunlight revealing something of an underwater street where young mullets cheerfully played. The sails of the trawlers, still offshore, struck by green and blue reflections of the sea and sky, resembled purple silk, planted there, like flowers in a garden, simply to enhance the beauty of the scene.

And even the man, beside the girl sifting through sand the same way he was sifting through his thoughts, felt calm, ready to draw strength from that pause for the remainder of the walk.

Part II

The Sin

14.

In May, the upstairs lodger gave notice that he would be arriving in a few days.

As a result, windows were flung open, mattresses beaten, and floors washed. The teacher offered to re-paper the little sitting room himself—since it really needed it—the way he'd done for his own room.

Marga protested, as usual, before finally agreeing. He then went to the upholstery shop in town where he purchased what was needed. Ola assisted in selecting the paper, recommending a brick color with golden flowers, and the upholsterer himself said it was an excellent choice: red withstands foxing from the sea air.

The sitting room furniture, stacked in the center of the room, was covered with a large canvas sail. Then the teacher fashioned a little paper hat like the one house painters use, and he put it on his head sideways, sparking Ola's mirth. She wanted one too, and so, with her curls looking blacker than ever poking out of that white beret, she became her grandfather's not entirely useless assistant.

She was the one who brought a container for preparing the glue from her mother's kitchen to the one upstairs, and at the proper moment produced a match from her pocket to light the stove, since the teacher didn't have one.

He laid out two long boards on the dining table, unrolled the paper face-down on top, and then began smearing the glue on. Suddenly a voice, not too high, but warm and with a restrained tone, filled the silence of the apartment illuminated by the sea's metallic light. He was singing like young workmen do on the job.

Ola dropped the paintbrush she'd been holding and laughed deliriously. Then, speechless, she looked at her grandfather as though he were a stranger. Was that really him singing? It really was him, and one would have said that as a young man he'd been a house painter, and now his entire happy history of carefree labor was returning with that voice and that song.

Everything around was animated by it and seemed to be listening, even the things hidden under the sail. In fact, Ola went to look at her doll, left on the couch, and it seemed to be opening its mouth to sing along. She scooped the doll up in her arms and next to her grandfather again, began accompanying him in falsetto, repeating the melody of his song.

But then he fell silent, as if snapping out of, before saying: "Go get Ornella."

Ornella was in the back room, washing the floor. She came immediately, in slippers without socks, arms bare, in a short skirt like a dancer's tutu. Her legs, covered in blonde peach fuzz and bare to her shiny pink knees, aroused a sense of wonder in the teacher. He'd never seen a woman's legs so long and powerful, and once again he thought of who knows what sort of mythical beast resembling a human female.

He had her take one end of the damp, gluey paper. Taking the other end, he climbed up the ladder leaning against the wall. Thus he began affixing the paper to the wall, aided skillfully enough by Ornella. When the first strip was in place, he stepped back to the opposite wall to see what the effect was. The girl and the young woman followed suit. But suddenly, as if stricken by the red of the paper, the woman flushed all over, and then her eyes widened before she blanched and bent over sideways. He barely caught her and supported her with all his might, leaning against the wall to avoid falling over himself.

"Get a chair, you fool!" he shouted at the girl who was laughing at seeing them in that awkward embrace.

Ola pulled the chair over, and he eased Ornella, who was collapsing like a rag doll, onto it. Then he told the girl to go get some water. Meanwhile, he supported the woman, who felt warm and in full bloom like some hothouse plant in his hands. That distinctive odor emanated from her white arms, smooth and green-veined on one side, covered with golden down on the other, from her barely-glimpsed bosom, snow-white as if swollen with milk, and from her undergarments—a scent like fresh grass cut and piled high that was beginning to ferment. A moment. And he felt a mysterious bewilderment, as if a group of adolescent memories were obstructing his brain, and he felt like he was back again in some cavernous place, a very long time ago, fighting with an ambiguous body that eluded and attracted him and possessed neither form nor substance, but still lived an intense life like a jellyfish at the bottom of the sea.

"Here's the water," said Ola softly, gasping in the face of Ornella's sudden loss of consciousness. "Is she dead? Ornella, wake up!" she shouted, pinching her knee.

More than the water splashed on her face and chest, it was that pinch that seemed to rouse Ornella. She put her hand on her knee, lifted her head and opened her eyes. When she appeared unwilling to give any explanation for her indisposition, the teacher reassured her:

"Up, up! It's just spring fever."

"Spring fever," she repeated pensively.

It all seemed to be over when she bolted up from the chair, but then she dropped back down as if her legs wouldn't support her. Doubling forward with her face in her lap, she bit her clothing and burst into tears. Ola flung herself on top of her, suddenly pale and scared, and began loudly sobbing as well.

These things pained the teacher. Witnessing that outburst of irrational heartache, as foolishly insane in the woman as in the girl, felt like witnessing an inexplicable phenomenon, but one that still had to have natural causes.

He gently pulled Ola off the woman and hugged her, noticing that she was burying her face into his chest to hide her shame. Ornella's sobs and shrieks gradually stopped, and little by little she lifted her head as if listening to a far-off sound. Then she forcefully blew her nose with her clothing and suddenly slipped away, creeping next to the wall, a bit hunched over.

The teacher didn't say a word to stop her. He just shook the girl and pulled away from her.

"Don't you see you're getting me all dirty with your snot?" he hollered.

And that was enough to dissipate the storm. Everyone went back to work.

The next day was a fever day, and Ornella stayed downstairs to keep an eye on Marga while the teacher completed decorating the sitting room. Once the upper border of the wallpaper had been applied, red with golden stripes that looked like brocade, what remained was to repaint the baseboard along the bottom of the walls. He'd provided for that as well, with a can of paint that looked like melted chocolate, which Ola delightedly inspected, getting paint all over her own fingers and little dress.

They were both still working at noon when Antonio came up to call them for lunch. Ola ran to him, arousing the usual faint jealousy in her grandfather. But her father held his hands up in front of him to protect himself from possible stains since he was wearing his new suit, the dark wool one that emphasized his athletic shoulders and brightened his complexion.

He'd been to the funeral of an old seaman who worked for him, but the emotion he displayed was instead one of glee. His broad, gleaming eyes sparkling with joy, along with his sharp profile and spirited mouth, reminded the teacher of a carefree adolescent coming home from some foray to the mountain woods with his friends, bearing a dead bird or a handful of mushrooms as a trophy. Since Ola was chasing and trying to grab him, he began leaping and hiding behind various furniture before finally ducking into the next room and shutting the door. But the girl circled around the apartment and snuck up on him, and laughter and shrieks like the chirping of swallows filled the silent rooms.

"He's still a boy," the teacher thought, happily putting the finishing touches on the wall, still deluding himself, like in the good old days, that Antonio would straighten up and become a devoted and faithful son and husband.

Even at the table, despite his occasional requests for them not to disturb the sick woman, the two continued laughing and joking. To account for his good spirits, Antonio said:

"If a deal that I started arranging today turns out well, oh, yes, we really will go on a trip to Jerusalem and then live upstairs without taking in any more of these intrusive boarders that come here because it's cheap and then try to act like barons."

He rubbed his hands, but then seemed to remember something upsetting.

"And I'll send for the most famous doctors in Italy to cure Momma."

Momma—that's what he called Marga with childlike fondness when she wasn't around.

"I think," the teacher observed, "that she just needs a change of scenery—take her up to the mountains for a while, now that it's starting to get hot."

"We'll go to the mountains, too, to the Engadin Valley that I know so well and where I even have an innkeeper friend. He made a fortune too, practically the same way that I did. Lunatics, both of us. He served as a customs officer with me and was making love to an innkeeper's daughter, unbeknownst to her parents. One fine day he got fired for who knows what sort of hot water. Anyway, he vanished for a while and then showed up at the inn dressed as a peasant woman applying for drudge work. And he got hired! And for three months he enjoyed himself with the daughter, until she confessed to her father that she was pregnant. They were thrown out of the inn, but in time her parents were moved to pity and forgave her. And now that the girl's father has died, my friend owns the inn. In fact, I should write him one of these days."

"Good, clever boys," the teacher said approvingly, even though he didn't much like hearing such anecdotes told in front of Ola.

Even Ornella was sullen as she served the meal, but due to something that seemed to concern her alone. Besides, no one paid her any attention, except perhaps the teacher. Every time she entered, he would glance at her out of a natural curiosity that he still hadn't clearly defined.

At the end of lunch, Antonio told her to go get a bottle of sparkling wine to celebrate the success of his big deal. When the bottle came, he stood and began laughing like he was already drunk, because in the hollow at the bottom of the bottle was a white spider that looked like silver.

"Luck and good fortune!"

He let the spider hurriedly escape its hiding place, and seeing it run confused back and forth on the back of the bottle, he bent down and helped it get to the floor.

"Go free! We all have a right to live!"

Ornella watched, and the irritation on her face dissolved into a slanted smile, mocking and almost cruel. In fact, as Antonio sat back down, she reached her foot out and squashed the spider. Only the teacher noticed the crime, and he said nothing.

The girl had become a bit sleepy, and the tales of youthful adventures that her father continued to recall didn't entertain her. She only began laughing again when he, after having drunk, pretended to play a violin, his head leaning towards the arm holding the invisible instrument, fingers plucking the no less invisible strings, voice imitating the sound. Then he pretended to set the instrument on the table and filled his glass once more.

"We'll take this one to Momma so she can drink to our big deal too."

That's when Ornella snapped. "But she doesn't want any, you know that."

His eyes flashed with anger. "Ornella! Take it to her anyway."

She obeyed but immediately returned holding the full glass with a thin layer of froth still quivering on top.

"Well, then, you drink it."

She never drank, at least not in the presence of others. But she drained the glass anyway, in three gulps, and the wine seemed to become fire under her skin which turned violently red.

The teacher didn't much like any of that either.

"Grouchy old schoolmaster Giuseppe," he said to himself when, after paying a quick visit to Marga and taking Ola to her little bed where she immediately fell asleep, he retired to his room as well, with the intention of taking a nap before getting back to work. "Why do you always have to be so disgruntled? You find a way to quibble with and criticize everything. Don't you remember that you were once young too and lived by the ancient proverb *youth is no virtue*? You know darned well what you did! And now you demand from others what you didn't do yourself."

Despite his docile thoughts, he didn't feel calm. He didn't want to sleep. He didn't want to read. Maybe he too was under the influence of the springtime, of that marine spring exploding like a violent storm.

The earth, reinvigorated by the breath of the sea, seemed to rise up on itself, swollen with grass and flowers, and every leaf, every flower shook with an almost crazed sense of joy. The roses that enflamed Ola's garden dropped their petals or fell to earth intact like they were drunk, and the midday wind tossed those petals, quivering like shreds of still living flesh, all the way into the schoolteacher's little room.

Closed up in that bedroom, more melancholy than ever in the splendor of the moment and the season, the man felt like a monk in his cell. The moment arrives when even the monk, after the fasting, sacrifices, abstinences, and ecstasies, feels his flesh reawaken and rebel, and his spirit plunge into the great despair of nothingness, a despair that wants to demonstrate the futility of pain itself.

"Schoolmaster Giuseppe, let's go outside, let's go and lose ourselves as well, among the grains of sand stirred up by the wind."

That's what he thought as he seemingly took his soul by the hand, like it was a little boy crying for no reason, to lead it outside.

He silently left his room. The kitchen remained in disarray since Ornella, taking advantage of everyone else's nap, was off possibly chatting with the farmers. Her absence irritated him, and he was vexed to an even greater degree when he saw the door to the little porch ajar. He was certain he'd locked it after having come back down with Ola and Antonio from upstairs. An instinct that was neither curiosity nor suspicion, but rather fear, spurred him to cautiously climb the stairs, and with some anxiety he recalled the day of the tour with Ola, the way she crept along the walls, the mystery that propelled them as if they were exploring an unknown temple.

"This house will be yours, Ola. All the light of the sea will be yours, when you're grown up and learn of love."

Everything rose up from his agitated heart as he climbed step by step, and he felt like he was climbing a perilous staircase, like in certain dreams.

He stopped on the landing. The door to the apartment was ajar as well, giving him the impression of an open mouth about to speak.

In fact, a voice did emerge, and then he grasped the meaning of the apprehension and subconscious instinct that had urged him on and led him there.

It was Ornella's voice.

15.

"That's the problem, that—that *Bulvin*. By now everyone knows that whore is going to be with you."

"Knock it off, Ornella," said the voice of Antonio, and it was calm, cheerful even, still tinged by the slight warmth of the sparkling wine, but like always, one heard an undertone of duplicity in it.

That must have irritated Ornella even more, because her voice rang louder, raucous and provocative, like the time when the teacher had heard her uttering indecent words with her companions.

"Are you going to be an angry beast about it? Well, you're already a beast—a cheating pig! But this time you're not getting off easy. You know I'm pregnant again. And this time I don't want to do that thing that animals won't even do and run the risk of ending up in prison."

"Stop it, Ornella, for your own good. You'll do what I tell you to do, and don't nag me about the rest of it. You know I'm a man of honor."

Ornella chuckled derisively, but he was docile, ready for anything, and he must have sealed her mouth with a kiss because she suddenly went quiet, and a sinister silence of guilt and vileness fell over their quarrel.

Then the teacher let himself slip down the stairs like a mortally wounded thief. He was leaving all the best blood of his life behind.

He headed to the gate and then turned around. But just the color of the house where Ola was sleeping while those two sinned upstairs hurt his eyes. He turned again and walked, down, down, all the way to the sand trenches where he dropped, despondent, perhaps like some old soldier under enemy fire back in the war days.

He had never been an impulsive man and didn't want to start being one in his old age, so he thought things over. The drama in which he felt like the central character loomed before him in its brutal simplicity, and he no longer had any doubt that Marga also knew about the betrayal and tolerated it out of a love for peace and quiet. Perhaps there's no such thing as a man who doesn't commit adultery, and in thousands of families, the deed occurs right in the house and sometimes takes on, as was happening now, a hint of incest. So then why was he painting this affair with such a tragic tone? After all, he'd had a feeling about it from the first day he arrived.

101

He knew why, and all the shadows that had briefly clouded that sensation of a new life found in Ola's love returned now, growing darker than ever, like a veil folded over and over again until no light could penetrate. That sandy niche where he lay was exactly where he had been sitting that day beside Ola, who was playing with shells and butterflies, when that sensation of a life waiting to be started all over again had seemed almost unbearable to him. And he remembered his prayer:

"Lord, I would willingly bear every multitude of sorrow you see fit to rain down upon me, if that would spare this young child beside me from ever being touched by evil."

And then he stood up, recognizing the will of God. And a host of sorrows swept over him, but didn't destroy him.

It was like threshing wheat in order to separate the clean, healthy grain from the chaff.

"I'm here," he said to himself, "prepared to do anything, even rip from my heart this final earthly joy, which is my love for the girl, if that's what it takes to save her."

He was one of those men who, once having made an informed decision, would allow nothing to change his mind, not even death. But just as he would look back when arriving at a bend in the road to gauge the distance he'd already traveled and the strength he had left to carry on, before getting up off the sand, the teacher reflected on his past and the reason he had come this far.

First he saw himself as a little boy in the modest house by the olive trees, in the austere shadow of the mountain. His father was the schoolmaster and an intrepid, passionate hunter in his free time. He never ate wild game, but would kill birds and animals out of a savage, primordial instinct. His mother made bread at home and worked the land like a peasant. She also pruned the vines and olive trees, and she knew the art of making wine and oil. She too, in her idle hours, cultivated a passion: she embroidered little tapestries in cross-stitch, with marvelous colors, tones, shadows, and precise borders.

One of those scenes, which she'd worked on years and years, was still kept in his suitcase because some quasi-superstitious impulse kept him from ever taking it out. He was afraid someone would steal it from him, bringing him bad luck.

His mother—like his father, for that matter—was thus a mix of coarseness and delicate kindness. He remembered that she never kissed him, but every night she would accompany him to his little bed and pray for him out loud. And he would feel her words tumbling onto his head like stars and flowers— the words of her prayer—but he would have preferred kisses.

And so, as a barely mature young man, finding himself embraced in the attention and caresses of a woman, he fell into her arms like a giddy little boy. She was a much older relative, and although it wasn't her first sin, when she realized that she was pregnant and the two couldn't continue their relationship, she hanged herself.

He still trembled at the memory, but didn't chase it away. Instead, he closed his eyes to more firmly capture it. He saw her again, the woman hanging from a beam like a large marionette. She'd covered her face. She'd dressed in red, with gold ribbons, the colors he liked. She'd dressed that way to marry death. Below her, on the floor, was a chair that seemed to have fainted in terror.

A three-year-old boy, fruit of her first sins, slept tranquilly in the one shared bed. She'd carefully tucked him in under the blankets and had covered his face with a handkerchief so that even asleep, he wouldn't *see*, and on the pillow, still bearing the imprint of her troubled head, she'd placed an olive branch.

"Peace, rest in peace," the man sobbed again, opening his eyes filled with pain and remorse.

He'd adopted the woman's son, and the years had passed. No one knew of his guilt. In fact, he came to be considered an austere and charitable man, practically a priest, as he was called by his pupils who respected him but didn't love him.

Meanwhile, his mother raised the boy like her real grandson. She alone suspected the truth and was grateful to the relative whose voluntary death had avoided family scandal and shame. The boy grew up handsome and overbearing. Knowing he wasn't the schoolteacher's son, he called him *uncle* and never once obeyed him.

After elementary school, he declared he wanted nothing more to do with formal education, and the teacher who longed to at least pass on his knowledge and teaching position to the boy began to agonize like a real father over his son's murky future.

But he'd accepted that paternity as penance for his sin and courageously faced his punishment in the boy's countenance.

This desire for atonement led his entire life to be straight and narrow, chaste. He felt the same impulses toward evil, the same carnal desires, and the same insurrections of the soul that every man did, but it felt like he was riding an untamed colt that was becoming more restrained and docile day by day.

At times he would have sort of a debate with God, and he always came out victorious. There was only one point on which God never yielded and he never insisted: regarding the boy who made him suffer without even letting himself be loved in return.

Even his elderly mother, after having suffered greatly when the boy ran away from home, died waiting for his return. In her wardrobe he found many things that had belonged to the boy: toys, clothes, drawings, baby teeth, and his first locks of hair tied with silk thread. Seeing them, the teacher finally cried, leaning against the open wardrobe like it was a wide-open door to a world of infinite pain and suffering. Then, from a distance, he began to love the young man, blaming himself for having raised him without love, only out of a sense of duty, and thus only out of selfishness.

His debates with God resumed until one day he came to his senses and told himself that it was all superstition. A man loves when he can and who he can, and it's all a mystery so immense and divine unto itself that even trying to explain it is a sacrilege.

He stood and walked along the road between the sandy shore and the little houses, the same route he'd taken with Ola the day after his arrival, through the disheveled tamarisks greeting and rejecting him from all sides, as if playing insouciantly while the wind gusted ever stronger. Even the alders, farther down, were all trembling, reflecting the motion and the sparkle of the waves below, beyond the frame of the beach.

The road continued on to who knows where—he'd never managed to walk all the way to the end and had the impression that it flanked the entire Adriatic. Because of this dreamlike atmosphere and because the sand trenches sheltered it from the wind, he preferred it to the others. The tepid sun lingered there with its intense sweetness, and on its grassy surface, barely furrowed by the wheels of the Emilia-Romagnan farmers' carts, and where the horse dung was greenish and clean, one walked as if on a velvety lane.

He preferred it. Along that road his woes dispersed, snatched up by the capricious branches of the tamarisks that would play with them before tossing them to the wind. And those furrows where the crocus flowers picked themselves back up, each with a drop of sunlight like an individual tear, and those few lonely butterflies that madly approached him, only to turn away as if not seeing in him what they were searching for—in short, it all reawakened a feeling of a second childhood in him.

The houses came to an end. The sea, after having appeared intermittently between the dunes, now was fully visible like a large plain covered with flax flowers. The road rose gently, and a line of soft clouds, above the alders towering over stunted tamarisks, seemed to repeat the waves' murmur. It was instead the trees that were murmuring, reminding him again of the religious hymns of his hometown, and he tried to repeat them too:

> *The sailor on the waves*
> *Invokes you, oh Lord...*

He immediately fell silent, though, struck by the sound of his voice that seemed to spring from the earth to be immediately swept away by the wind. But the image of the sailor amidst the rough waves invoking the Lord didn't forsake him as he continued walking with some difficulty uphill, against the wind, like a boat in peril. Then he suddenly stopped, with a sense of relief, almost as if he'd made it home.

Behind the veil of a gate's lattice, a house did in fact rise up in front of him, gray with age and neglect.

It was the Ontani house, the cursed house.

After all, it wasn't the first time he'd stopped to look at it, and the thought of all those rooms vacant for years, while he was forced to live in a tiny room as dark and damp as a basement, tethered him to the lattice of the gate with the same fascination of children leaning over the edge of a well to gaze at a subterranean sky a thousand times more attractive than the real one.

A tiny old woman, dressed in black, hunched forward as if searching for something on the ground, appeared at the back of the clearing and proceeded towards the gate. He recognized the little old lady "who steals children" and sensed that she had seen him as well and was coming down to ask him something. In any case, he moved away from the lattice and headed back.

Now the wind was at his back. He felt it blowing into every opening of his jacket, and although he saw trees swollen with green and grapevines blue with copper sulphate, he thought it felt like winter.

Such a long, long time had passed since he'd left Ola's house! Tired, he again collapsed on the roadside, and it felt like the sun covered his knees with a warm cloth. It was a bit more of the good Lord's warmth, a bit of warmth in death.

And so the old woman who'd come out of the cursed house reached him walking along with a strange gait—she would plant one foot on the ground and then drag the other along, with only the tip of her big toe in the worn-out shoe that occasionally slipped away from her, seemingly trying to hide itself in the grass.

That foot must have been painful, because an expression of suffering furrowed her face. When she arrived next to the teacher, though, her eyes lit up and her entire body straightened. It seemed he was what she had been searching for, the cure for her ills. She looked him right in the eye and greeted him with the question:

"Good day. Where's *your* little girl?"

Just being able to talk about the girl dissipated the shadows and the cold surrounding him.

"Sleeping," he replied softly, as if not to wake her. "Do you know her?"

"Who doesn't know her? Don't you recall that I saw you together in the piazza? I also know her father, Antonio De Nicola."

He thought of asking what people said about Antonio, in town, and if they were familiar with his overindulgences, but what was the point? Didn't he already know them better than anyone?

"The girl is pretty and robust," the old woman said in the meantime, as if to comfort him. "And she must be very kind. I like children very much, and perhaps that's why they say that I steal them. I really would steal some, if I could, and if I could provide well for them. But they say it with a different meaning. Mothers say it to keep their little ones from coming up here, to a place that is certainly very isolated."

The old woman smiled derisively in the face of his benevolence.

"Do you believe it? Still, it is true that I once tried to steal a baby boy, in our early days here. My son doesn't want to take a wife, and I would so love the company of grandchildren. Those innocent creatures," she continued, as the teacher stared at her with both worry and unease. "They protect against evil and bless the place where they live. And I'm afraid of staying in that cursed house of murder. Even my son is starting to believe that it's under an evil spell. We've been oppressed by misery since we came here. At night we hear strange sounds, inside the house, like the sons are killing their father again, and then the dog took ill, but from a mysterious sickness—at night he would whimper wide-eyed as if he *saw* and *heard*. He seized onto my son's pantleg and led him to the gate, undoubtedly wanting us to leave. He died yesterday, and my son cried. Then he buried him in the back of the field, and today he went looking for a friend of his to ask if he wanted to take over for us, looking after the house."

The schoolteacher lifted his head energetically.

"Why don't you look around here, for a caretaker?"

"See if you could find one for me. I can't even find another dog in this Jewish town."

He looked down again. He barely knew the town, but he did know that everyone worked, on land and on the sea, owners of fishing boats and properties large and small. Everyone was making money, perhaps a little too attached to it in fact, like Israelite merchants, and even the poorest soul would be ashamed of simply looking after a house under sequestration.

"Up there it's not easy either," added the old woman, pointing to a far-off place. "People don't like staying in someone else's house, in someone else's town."

"And they're right," he said, without looking up. It seemed he was no longer paying attention to her, fully immersed in his own thoughts, as strange and muddled as hers. But they gradually took shape, coming together, distilling into one sole thought.

"What has to be done, to watch after the house?" he asked at last.

"Next to nothing. Just keep an eye out so that no one—thieves or relatives of the boys who killed their father—breaks the seals or gets into the house any other way."

"Where's the caretaker's quarters?"

"Attached to the main house. Come and take a look."

He instinctively moved to stand up, but then firmly shook his head, saying:

"I'm too old. Otherwise, I'd go."

"I'm the one who's old," she exclaimed, delighted to have found what she'd been looking for. "And my son is always ill, but he still easily managed to watch over the house."

"But the fields, who farms them?"

"They're rented out to some farmers—all we have is a little piece of land behind the house. Then there's the pay. Not much, six *lire* a day, but it's something. As soon as my son returns, I'll send him to see you, so—"

"No, no, Old Woman," he said, bewildered, "I was kidding."

16.

But just as a joke, even an unintentional one, can lessen a deep pain, he felt comforted. He resumed his walk.

He increasingly felt God's presence beside him. Wasn't it perhaps God who had sent the old woman to offer him a refuge for his penance? First, though, he needed to fulfill his duty, without delay, in regard to Antonio. And the house from which he'd fled in despair and revulsion now was drawing him back like a temple where one repents, prays, and sacrifices.

He found Antonio preparing to leave, adjusting his tie and the brim of his hat in front of the dining room mirror.

Seeing him from behind, that strong, agile back and powerful neck reminded him, like Ornella's figure did, of some unknown being closer to an animal than a human. A superior man generally has a weak, imperfect body—the flesh weighs on the spirit in one way or another, so that the spirit tries to defeat it, to overcome it.

"Antonio, where is Ornella?" The question, although spoken softly and prudently, immediately alarmed Antonio who rigidly turned around. But the other man's appearance was so tired and defeated that he felt reassured, and with solicitude he replied:

"Do you need something?"

"I need to speak with you. Come with me, to my room."

There they could speak calmly. Things in the greenish shadows surrounding them were apparently pretending to sleep in order to not disturb their conversation. Besides, everything seemed simple and clear to the teacher now, and he had no intention of getting lost in useless words.

"Sit," he said, pulling out the chair in front of the desk where a string of beads left by Ola snaked its way among his letters. And while Antonio pulled the chair closer, obeying like a little boy, the teacher hid the beads under a letter, not because he was afraid of suffering, but because he suddenly felt that he was being guided not only by a desire to save the girl from the depravity around her, but by a universal inclination for good.

"Listen," he said, as he listened to his own words as well, speaking with the humble tone of a man trying to defend himself rather than offend someone else, "without meaning to, I overheard your conversation with Ornella today."

Antonio seemed neither shocked nor concerned. In fact, his womanizer's fatuous, derisory smile reflexively raised his upper lip as he waited for the teacher to continue. The teacher didn't continue. He'd seen that smirk and sensed the futility of his battle.

"That damn girl!" Antonio finally burst out. "She probably left the door open on purpose. For this, for this!" he repeated, angrily removing and replacing his hat.

"And why didn't you close it? Maybe it would've been better. Yes, better to ignore evil than to pointlessly fight it."

"Do you really think," Antonio said cynically, "that this is her first time? And what man could pass up such an opportunity? Let he who is without sin cast the first stone."

And the teacher truly felt like he'd been struck by the very same stone he was trying to cast. But he didn't stop.

"You shouldn't sin in your own home, your daughter's home. Not here, or anywhere, for that matter—sin is still sin, wherever it's committed. And you shouldn't bring suffering unto your wife, who possibly knows everything and tolerates it all for the girl's sake. It may be that I'm not fit to cast the first stone, but that's precisely why I'm telling you that, one of these days, certain things will exact a steep price."

Antonio appeared shaken. Looking down, he smoothed his hat without reacting. He only asked: "Is it Marga who's making you say this?"

"Antonio! Your wife would sooner die than open her heart to another living soul. But even her laughter exudes pain."

"Marga doesn't love me," said Antonio, scowling. "She only loves her dead husband."

"That's not true! She takes shelter in her memories the way a wounded doe hides in her lair. But that's not important either. The main thing is that the air needs to be cleared here, because Marga's behavior only adds to the infection. The air needs to be cleared, purified," he repeated, spreading his hands and shaking them like fans. "For the girl, if not for you. Do you understand?"

"What does the girl know about it?"

"The girl, if she keeps breathing this air, will go astray like you, and one day, when she sees the pain in your eyes over her perdition, she won't hesitate to say: *You were the one who taught me to sin.*"

Antonio snapped like a twig bent too far.

"No, no, not her. If I'm this way, it's because that's how I was born. We're born... We're born... My mother was like Ornella."

At that moment an iron chain seemed to approach the two men, suddenly catapulting them both into the same abyss of shame and dread.

With a whisper the teacher asked: "So you admit that you sinned?"

"I do. But I'm not alone. Many are worse than me."

"We're all awash in good and evil, but the latter must be defeated, Antonio. Steel—even steel—can be tempered and forged into a sword by those wishing to vanquish their enemy."

Antonio stood there like a servant awaiting orders, cruelly tormenting his felt hat as if it were a live animal. At last he said:

"Tell me what I must do."

"You must immediately send that girl away and then provide for her and her baby."

"And then?" Antonio sadly persisted.

"And then God will help you, if your intentions are good," the teacher said, but he too was overwhelmed by a feeling of loss at the thought of what came next.

And this fog never lifted again. He sensed that Antonio, despite appearing compliant, was eluding him, slipping from his grasp like a cat that appears docile but is unable to renounce its feral instincts.

17.

He took a late walk with Ola. Rather than lifting his spirits, though, her company sharpened his discomfort. His thoughts kept racing home, where he felt like he'd left a gravely wounded Antonio.

Ola was pulling him towards town, where there were people and noise, but he headed towards the lonely roads where their footsteps died in the thick grass and the sky again offered his eyes the reflection of the deadly solitude hollowing out his heart.

Ola was getting bored. She bent over two or three times to pick little flowers and look at insects, but she no longer beckoned to her grandfather with her cries of wonder. She was caught up in a secret thought of her own. Once she lingered so long that he, having continued on, turned to call her. She didn't reply, didn't budge, disobedient and taciturn until he finally came back and threatened to slap her.

And so they became enemies. "It's better that way," he thought bitterly, "since one of these days we'll have to part ways."

Seized and pulled along by his hand, she looked up at him, studying him closely, like the first day they met. It felt like she was with a different man, a different grandfather than the one before. Bored and tired, she abruptly asked:

"What songs did you know when you were a little boy?"

"I knew plenty," he replied gruffly. "Now I'm old and don't remember them anymore."

"Not even the one about the sailor on the waves?"

"Not even that one," he said, harsh and obstinate, but suddenly he heard the sound of an organ from faraway. Where? Faraway, beyond the plain, beyond the sea—accompanied by a religious hymn. The feeling was so strong that he stopped to listen.

"Don't you hear anything?" he asked the girl. "Don't you hear some far-off music?"

"Yes, I hear it," she said, willingly accepting the power of suggestion.

They both stood there on the lonely road, amidst the grass and the playful tricks of the sun and shadows, as if in a magical circle between dream and madness.

18.

The days passed and Ornella was still in the house, more taciturn and patient than ever in the face of Marga's unjust, exasperating reprimands. Even Antonio's mood darkened, and not even the amber wine from the old bottles managed to lighten it. Moreover, he was always out of the house and would return scowling, as if business were going bad. He would barely eat and drink before leaving again.

One day he returned with a famous doctor who had a bearded face and the mysterious air of a wizard. It was a fever day, and Marga resigned herself to his examination but didn't answer the scientist's questions, and when he declared that she needed a change of scenery and climate, and that they should take her to the hills or possibly the mountains, she turned her face toward the pillow and closed her eyes, tired and hostile.

When they were out in the little dining room, the great doctor said that the apparently strange case was actually quite simple: her old malaria fevers were being exacerbated by a pathological case of hysteria.

"On her good days, does she work?" he asked.

"Too much even. She doesn't stop for a minute."

"That's bad. Is she depressed?"

"No, not as far as I know," Antonio replied, but his eyes avoided the teacher's.

The doctor didn't leave any prescription in exchange for the nice envelope of money Antonio nonchalantly handed him. He only repeated his advice to get Marga out of the house, up high, as far away as possible.

The schoolteacher thought about his town and the house he might be able to get back, but when Antonio said that he already knew where to take Marga and the girl—to some distant relatives of hers—he looked down and left the room.

He made his way back towards the house with the alders. That visit by the foreign doctor seemed rather mysterious to him, like a trick arranged by Antonio to get Marga and the girl out of the house. Why? The murkiest, most unspeakable thoughts led his mind astray, but of course when one is overwhelmed by sin, anything seems possible. And he felt like he no longer had the courage even to keep confronting the man whom he'd once hoped to make his son. He felt that an unknown force was placing that tragedy in front of him, that it was removed from him, but seemingly radiating from him, and that only another force, his inner strength, could undo it. In a nutshell, he thought that it was all retribution for his still unatoned-for sin, and that only by suffering, being humiliated, and sacrificing the joy of living, could things be brought to good resolution.

And once again, like a moth drawn to a flame, he went and banged against the gate of the cursed house. The place aroused the same fascination in him as it did in imaginative children. But it was also the sort of backdrop for his secret pain that he was searching for, a grim, opaque setting where the contours of his suffering would stand out better. The penitent was seeking out a cave in which to atone.

In truth, there in the lonely garden, the spring was casting its veil of joy even now. The trees, swollen and green, echoed with birdsong, and the benches and tables, washed by the last rain, appeared brand new.

And there, as if herself drawn by a secret call, the old woman appeared at the end of the path. Hunched over, she was looking at the ground as usual, but when she noticed the teacher, she tried to straighten up. With one foot leading and the other dragging, she raced down to the gate and opened it without further ado.

Then he recalled having promised to return and went in. After closing the gate, she led him to see the caretaker's quarters.

19.

Abutting the main house, it was a long room which once must have served as a coach-house or some such. Half was as high as the roof, whose red tiles were visible through the beams. The other half was covered by a loft accessible by means of a narrow staircase.

"Up there is where my son sleeps," the old woman explained. "There are even sheets that were included with the furniture."

"Nice furniture," thought the teacher, looking around.

In the corner under the loft, the old woman's bed was covered by fabric that looked like a gunny sack. Piles of old sprouted potatoes and dried sweetcorn leaves accompanied the few other grimy, wobbly pieces of furniture that testified to the fact that human beings lived there. Then the walls, raw and blackened with smoke, would have brought to mind the primitive kitchens of well-off tenant farmers were it not for the filth, disarray, and barn stench that lent the entire environment an inhuman air. The sole compensation for all that wretchedness was a large fireplace with a stove under the same hood, and the burning fire created something of a background of hope, offering the prospect that the hovel was indeed habitable.

On the flame a black pot was boiling, its dancing lid allowing the scent of garlic-seasoned beans to escape—a humble, genuine smell that reminded the man of the savory aromas of Marga's kitchen and Ola's little fingernail tapping on the shiny enamel of the pot, auguring a good dinner. And he didn't drive the memory away, even though it pained him. After all, penance isn't penance if it isn't interwoven with sacrifices large and small.

20.

Towards evening he went in to see Marga. She was without fever, but more exhausted than usual, the cadaverous bluish pallor of her face rendered more sinister in the reddish glow of twilight.

"That doctor," she asked with her sleepy voice, "what did he say?"

"He said nerves were part of it and that you need to rest and take care of your spirit."

That's what he said, believing he knew more about it than the doctor, but Marga's spectral smile displaying teeth like in a young woman's skull immediately disheartened him.

Even from that side of things, words were pointless. He regained hope, however, when she said:

"But there's nothing wrong with my spirit. And I do want to follow the doctor's advice. What if we went to your town, Papa? I've wanted to for so long."

"Why didn't you ask earlier? Now it's too late. I sold the house and wouldn't know where to go."

"It doesn't matter, Papa," she said, suddenly resigned again. "I'll go wherever Antonio takes me. Won't you come with us, Papa? That way, Antonio could stay on here, tending to the house with Ornella until our return."

The teacher looked at her. She kept her eyelids lowered, as if avoiding him, and he had the urge to raise them with his fingers, those eyelids as oppressive as gravestones, and to yell so that everyone could hear: *Get up, woman! Get up and walk!*

"Marga," he said harshly, "I'm not coming with you. I'm leaving here soon."

"Why? Why?"

Between those two sincere, fervent yelps, there was a brief silent period during which the glimmer illuminating the pillow seemed to move, rising towards the wall, and her face was lost in black shadow.

"She's dead—her soul's dead," thought the teacher.

Nevertheless, he felt a violent urge to confess to her, just as he would to a dead man he'd offended in life. It was his turn to close his eyes as he spoke. His voice sounded murky to him, and yet, at times, resonant like a note from an oboe, with a weeping tremulousness.

"Marga, I came here with the hope of spending my remaining days with you and perhaps renewing my life the way an old, dilapidated boat, after so many hardships, hopes to return to port and be refitted. But I see that that's not possible. Perhaps the fault is mine. I realize more and more every day that between me and you—between my way of thinking and living and yours—there's an insurmountable conflict. And so I can't help but annoy you, and for my part, get upset and suffer needlessly."

"Please don't speak," he added, sensing her agitation. "I've told you before that you're intelligent and you know what I mean. I also know all about you, even if you don't talk much. Remember, Marga, that first evening when I arrived? Even then I understood all the murkiness swirling in your life and Antonio's. Now, though, things are getting worse. Out of self-interest and a lack of religion, you are all on the brink of the worst of sins, that of killing an innocent creature before it's born. I, however, have no intention of associating with you any longer, not even out of consideration for the little girl who is breathing this immoral air and who will end up falling into ruin herself."

Marga had pressed her face into the pillow and was sobbing. Suddenly she turned towards him, shaking her head to free herself from her veil of hair. She tried to speak, but only a moan passed through her lips.

"Words are useless, Marga. Deeds are far better. Besides, don't think that I'm here just to pointlessly preach morality to you. I've sinned too. I've even committed a sin similar to the one which I now wish to avoid: A woman, the mother of your husband, took her own life because of me. She was pregnant and knew that I had no intention of marrying her. I took her first child home with me. He wasn't mine, but I wanted to make him my son. Doing so, I believed I was making amends. Instead, it was only the seed of my true atonement. That true atonement begins now, and I fully accept it if means that all of you can be saved. Don't cry, Marga, don't cry. Instead, get up. Like Christ said to Lazarus: 'Get up and walk.'"

The woman was crying, silently now, hiding her face behind her black shroud of hair.

"I like your tears," he said, standing without opening his eyes. "They're like the first rain after a long drought. And you'll get up and teach your daughter what I've been wanting to teach her—that in order to be truly happy, one needs to live a pure life and follow Christ's laws. You'll do it. If not today, tomorrow."

Part III

—◆◇◆—

The Penance

21.

The next day Marga and Ola, accompanied by Antonio, left for a town in the Apennines, where certain relatives of theirs owned a house in the middle of a forest of chestnut trees. The teacher went to the station with them, carrying Ola along the boulevard. Thinking of the trip and the new things she'd see, the girl wasn't very upset about their separation.

"I'll write to you," she said seriously, to comfort him. "Then I'll bring you plenty of chestnuts, as big as my fist. With the burrs, too. Feel how prickly they are."

She pinched his face, and they shared a final laugh together.

For that matter, he was almost happy himself. He'd resolved his inner dilemma and superstitiously believed that on the scales of life, suffering would be counterbalanced by the good which could arise from it.

He went home and spent three days alone with Ornella, never saying a single word to her about the matter that concerned them all. He had a mysterious fear of her, as if she were a devious being who, at the slightest provocation, could transform herself into a monster. At night he locked his bedroom door, and during the day he would go out to eat, afraid she might poison him.

On the evening of the third day, he packed his suitcase, and a few minutes before Antonio returned, left him a handwritten note saying he'd been compelled to leave. He said goodbye to Ola's toys. He said goodbye to the dog who was lurking nervously around him, perhaps sensing the man's intentions. Finally, he looked for the cat. At last finding him curled up, asleep on the corner of the sofa in Marga's room, he stopped to contemplate the animal.

The only paw visible was the one wrapped around the bottom of the cat's face, where the silvery strands of his right whiskers poked out. His pink ear, folded back, resembled a seashell full of golden seaweed. And his tail, with its brown and yellowish rings, nicely arranged around the front of his tightly curled body, completed the harmonious circle. His belly moved with his breath, and when the brown fur spread, revealing the white underneath, it really looked like that was where the breath was coming out. And that rhythmic rise and fall of the tabby's fine belly reminded him of the rolling waves of the sea.

22.

The paperwork to change caretakers for the sequestered house was already completed, so the teacher went there directly for the handover.

The old woman sold him, at an exorbitant price, their leftover provisions, four egg-laying hens, and one rooster whose only thought was to enjoy life. As a bonus, she gave him a bit of coal and showed him how to always keep the fire alive: he just needed to bury nicely glowing embers in the hot ash. When she and her son had gone, wobbling under the weight of their loads, both of them small and misshapen like twilight gnomes, he closed the gate and peered through the lattice. Beyond the grassy road, the already gray horizon looked like the wall of an immense prison.

Now alone, he felt a sense of loss, the way the thought of death provokes terror because it means the end of everything. He wanted to cry, to lean against the gate and kiss the lattice where Ola's tiny fingers had slipped through the slats. Then he thought that the old woman truly had stolen the girl from him, and he regretted having run away, which now seemed like a pointless, cowardly act.

"A man's true strength lies in fighting evil head-on, with brutality even. I should have spoken more clearly to Marga and Antonio, forcing them to fulfill their duty."

Then he shivered and headed back toward the sad lair where he'd taken refuge like a wounded animal. He walked around the big house, black and opaque against an already sparkling starry sky. The fire was burning in his room, and that glimmer reawakened a sense of purpose in his life. He felt obligated to never let the fire die, that he'd promised it to someone. He added some wood.

Hope returned to his heart. He was comforted by the very disorder and filth that surrounded him. After all, he felt like the caretaker of a dead world, the house where the sons had killed their father, and he was surrounded by a whole world that needed organizing and cleaning.

23.

That very evening, while he was feeling completely alone on earth, he received a visit. It was the elderly farmer who rented the field belonging to the house. He introduced himself respectfully, straw hat in hand, and after timidly asking if he could be of service in some way, he too began complaining about the bane that truly seemed to weigh on that estate.

"Four of us came here—me, my brother, my wife, and a cousin of hers. We all got along, and at first, everything flourished. Then my wife died, and her cousin left because there was no longer any reason for him to stay with us. Only my brother Gesuino and I are left, and we work like dogs, barely able now to eke out the rent for the field. Everything goes wrong. Even the hens have stopped laying eggs. To top it all off, my brother and I bicker constantly. Actually, being a decent man, I'm sure you'll forgive us even if you see us coming to blows."

"Goodness! Why do you do that?"

"Just because we feel like it. It never used to happen. Gesuino is a good man, too good, religious and taciturn. His chest is covered with sacred images, he's always praying, and he believes in spirits, fairies, and plenty of other crazy things. But when it comes to speaking ill, he has a tongue like a skewer. I'm not evil either. And we do love each other. Still, we're always fighting. He says it's witchcraft."

"Are there no women, in your house?"

He waved his hand as if casting out evil spirits.

"After the death of my wife, we took in a relative. She robbed us blind, and it was she who began sowing discord between us, so one day I chased her off with a stick. Then we took in a sort of servant. This one didn't steal and didn't meddle in our affairs, but she stayed out with men all day, finally becoming a whore and catching a filthy disease that civility prevents me from mentioning. Miserable by then, Gesuino and I decided to live without women. Life is bad, but better than with strange, unknown women. Besides, Gesuino has learned to do everything. He even sews, but that takes up a lot of his time."

"Why don't the two of you remarry?"

The farmer peered up at him with his sad but malicious little green eyes, already buried in wrinkles.

"I'd like to, yes, but I'd like a young wife, and one with some means, but I'm afraid of them, with few exceptions."

He crossed his fingers and laughed. The other man thought that the farmer was pulling his leg a bit.

"What about your brother?"

"Oh, well, he's taken a vow of chastity. He hates women and runs away when he sees one. But then, he runs away from men too. This evening he didn't want to come with me to greet you, and you'll see that you won't be able to speak to him twice in a year."

"All right, you and I will be better friends, then."

"Don't think that I'm the sort of man who loves chit-chat either," the farmer immediately assured him, "but sometimes one needs to vent. And if you don't vent with men, where do you? They say you were a teacher, and so you know a lot of things. A lot of things..." he repeated pensively. "The old woman who was here told me: 'When you need advice, go to him because he's very wise.'"

"What does the old woman know of me? If I were really such a wise man, I wouldn't be here. At any rate, though, if you ask my opinion, I'll gladly provide it, just as you can feel free to give me yours."

"And if you need something," continued the other man, encouraged and heartened, "don't hesitate to ask. The old woman may have spoken ill of us because in fact she didn't get along with Gesuino, and her son demanded that we keep watch while he was off somewhere, and he was always off somewhere. Recently though, both of them had become... strange. They would *see*, that is to say, they *thought* they saw the ghost of the man killed by his sons. We would laugh, even though my brother somewhat believes in that foolishness. You certainly don't believe it, though."

"The dead are dead," said the teacher, "and it's the ghosts of the living that should frighten us."

"Well said! But now I'll take my leave and make my apologies. Early tomorrow morning I'm going into town; if you need something, feel free to ask. That's the other reason I came."

"Well, you could buy me some bread. And there's another thing I must ask of you: don't speak of me, don't say that I'm here."

With two fingers the farmer pressed his lips together, and his eyes reminded the teacher of the way Ola's dog looked when he was being petted. He took comfort, then, since it seemed that Providence had sent him, via the material assistance of this simple man, the solace that the proximity of one soul lends to another.

From the very first night he did his duty. He thought he heard a noise and went around the house to look. Everything was calm, and the moonlight in fact lent the silent, dead place a spectral glow. Just in front of one of the marble tables, the teacher thought he saw a shadow. It was the shadow of a bush; he saw it clearly, but a shiver of mystery still pulsed in his blood. He remembered Ola's tiny hand squeezing his, and thought that mankind's justice wasn't sufficient to wipe out evil. He returned to his bed but couldn't get back to sleep. He heard dogs barking in the distance and mice walking on the roof. Even the hens huddled on a perch in the back of the room would every so often cluck—a faint cluck of dreams. He lit the lamp and tried to read, but the poor light strained his eyes, and what he read didn't penetrate into his soul like other times. Then he put the light out and surrendered to his memories, especially the ones he wanted to escape, the same way a mother offers her breast to a restless toddler in the night, even though she knows it could do more harm than good.

But his insomnia was drawn out, insistent, and only at dawn, when he was expecting to get up, did a violent, turbid sleep filled with bad dreams swoop down on him like a nightmare.

24.

When he awoke, he saw that the farmer had set the bread on the window ledge next to a bucket of fresh water. Such kindness moved him.

"What must they think of me? That I came here just to sleep?"

He began to work. He fed the hens and set out to clean the room, a difficult task because the old woman had left only the worn-out stub of a broom and not even a rag. But he remembered the farmer's offer and went to ask to borrow a broom. The two brothers, who resembled each other to a remarkable degree, both short and burly and with reddish hair, were working in the field in front of the house. The old man was pulling smooth, round potatoes that looked like yellow marble eggs from the earth that had already grown a bit hard with the first of the hot weather. The teacher stopped to look on. That human nutriment springing from the dark seclusion of the earth seemed a miracle to him. The farmer, however, was complaining:

"They're so few and small, they don't even replace the seed potatoes."

He asked the teacher to accept some anyway, and he took them, looking towards Gesuino who had barely returned his greeting. Gesuino didn't seem to pay any attention to him, but once the teacher had walked away with the broom and potatoes, he heard the two brothers quarreling.

The work made his morning seem short and almost cheerful. He took the sweetcorn leaves, the rotted potatoes, and all the useless or broken items that cluttered up the room out to the farmers' manure heap. He also took the furniture outside, to wash and disinfect it in the sun, along with the mattress and bedcovers. He was amazed to see that the sheets, which the old woman had changed the day before, were clean. In exchange, up in the loft, where he climbed with what was for him an astonishing agility, he found a pile of dirty bedsheets.

This loft also made for a little room, with a bed and a trunk good for a table or chair. A small, narrow window let in some light and looked down on the farmers' field. Once he'd cleaned up there, the teacher climbed down and began sweeping the room. The dust and debris from the floor danced around him, practically mocking him. The more he swept, the more there was, and every so often he stepped outside to spit and blow his nose. He thought of Ola—if only she were there to laugh at him and help him! No, no. He swallowed his perturbation along with the dust, and returned to his labors like a convict who'd looked through the bars of his cell to see the far-off sky for a moment. When he'd finished cleaning the floors and walls, where spiderwebs rained down, covered with flies that had been dead for years, he thought about eating something. He went to look in the cage half full of straw where the hens, according to the old woman, laid four eggs a day, but he only found two, one covered with black speckles, which was the appealing one, the other being white and warm, as if already cooked.

He contented himself with that one and dunked his bread in the egg with hedonistic joy, the way Ola would dunk cookies into cream.

Then he resumed his chores. When the furniture was washed and put back and the crude bed remade, he felt like he'd landed, after a laborious crossing, in a new port. And like all new arrivals, he opened his suitcase.

The first thing he removed was the alarm clock which had followed him from his hometown. It still ran, indifferent to everything that wasn't its duty—keeping time. Positioned in the middle of the still damp table, it continued undaunted, already the master of the location and the space around it.

The teacher felt enlivened, as if he'd rediscovered a companion in his solitude. But what most comforted him was the roll of canvas, yellowed around the edges, that during his stay in Marga's house he'd never taken out of the suitcase. It was the small tapestry his mother had embroidered. He unrolled it on the table, holding it down with his fingers before standing up to better see it from a distance.

The scene depicted a barren beach. The sand, embroidered with raw silk thread, marked the foreground. After that came the greenish band of sea against the bluish-gray background of the sky. On this landscape, where just three lines indicated a deep, spacious vastness, two figures were walking. Yes, he really seemed to see them walking, feet lifted, footsteps behind them in the sand. One figure represented a bald man with a long tunic tied at the waist and rope sandals. He was carrying a bundle, walking ahead of a woman taller than he, holding in her arms a baby completely covered by a dark cloth (it must have been a baby by the way she was holding it). She was dressed in red, with rope sandals, her head wrapped in braids admirably rendered with golden yellow silk.

On the empty bottom edge of the canvas, embroidered in black silk, appeared the title:

The Flight into Egypt

With four tacks the small tapestry was secured to the wall above the bed, and it seemed to brighten up the entire room.

The top cover of the bed, the one that looked like a gunny sack, was spread out on the floor like a rug, leaving only by the reasonably clean, fringed white blanket, which the old woman had kept folded up under the pillow, to cover the sheets.

25.

When everything was in order, the teacher went back to return the farmers' broom. Without meaning to, he heard them exchanging harsh words as if they'd done nothing else all day long, and he had to laugh. Noticing him, they fell silent, and the old man stood to greet him respectfully.

"Here's the broom," he said, leaning it there. "Thank you. And thank you also for your potatoes—they were as good as the butter."

"We haven't tasted them yet. Today the cook," said the farmer, winking at his brother, "is in a foul mood."

"I know. You're angry with me, Gesuino? You have reason to be because I've been coming too often, bothering you and wasting your time. But in return, I can also be of use to you. Come and eat with me tonight. I don't have much at home, but what little I do have, I'll find a way to multiply, like Jesus did. But you need to get the wine for me."

"The wine we have," said the old man, while his brother continued hoeing, frowning and silent. "It's very light, but good."

"No, no. I want a generous wine that strengthens the blood. There is, I believe, an inn here at the crossroads. If it's not a bother, go and get two flasks of wine."

"Jesus and Mary! You want to send us to the next world!"

"We'll go there together, if anything," he said, giving the man the money for the wine. "What do you say, Gesuino? Would you answer, please? Are you coming or not?"

"Of course!" grumbled Gesuino, without turning his head.

"Oh, we've finally heard the sound of your voice! And now, it's time to prepare the banquet."

26.

The hasty invitation didn't daunt him. Among other things, the old woman had sold him an entire mountain ham, wheat, preserves, and cheese. To make a good impression, all he needed was willingness and competence, and if the latter was in short supply, he possessed the former in spades.

And so he set water to boil while he pulled down the ham which hung like a lamp attached to a rope in the middle of the room, safe from the mice. He set it on the table and looked at it, turning it around and around to find a good place to start. The right flank looked good to him, but he quickly realized it was too lean, and he needed fat for various reasons. Then he tried the opposite side, and beneath the coarse, salty skin, appeared the white and red of the fat and meat.

The knife was sluggish, though, unwilling to cut a thin slice, and so he sharpened it with another small knife. The two blades flashed and clanged in a savage duel, but with bursts of joy. And now the big knife, blazing with victory, silently slipped back into the patient ham, and this time the slices came off diaphanous and wide. The teacher looked at them against the light, like swatches of expensive fabric. The fat resembled white velvet and the lean meat mahogany-colored damask.

Placing a big rose of these slices on a round tray, he cut more from the fat side, haphazardly tossing those unfortunate slices onto the cutting board, where the knife loudly lashed out, finally reducing them to pulp. The already boiling pot was moved to the edge of the stove to make room for the small black skillet with the lard tossed in, given the comforting companionship of little chunks of butter, onion, and garlic, and everything began frying, complaining softly at first, then loudly, until the tomato puree's dense blood mixed in, seemingly transforming the pain into joy.

With the water back on to boil, the teacher pulled down the big pasta board, clean and almost virginal in its white wooden nudity. Recalling the motions of women carrying out this chore, he poured a small mountain of wheat in the middle, using his finger to make something like the crater of a volcano. It truly resembled a volcano, that little mountain, when he poured the boiling water into the hole. Steam rose, the heap collapsed, and he plunged his hands in like he was trying to support and rebuild it.

The flour, however, escaped from all sides, and that which was already soaked stuck to his fingers with spite and vindictiveness. Soon his hands looked like they were enclosed in white wool gloves, and the flour that was desperately escaping the board spilled onto the front of his suit.

It was a difficult moment. Despondent, he looked at his jacket, not daring to touch himself with those monstrous fingers. Then he remembered that nothing in life scared him anymore, and slowly, slowly, using one hand, he liberated the other from the pasta covering. With both he gathered the scattered army of flour onto the center of the board, poured more water, and then his fingers proudly squeezed the rebellious material into a compact form.

And by dint of sighs and brute force and pain in the palm of his right hand, the hard, wooden pasta was rendered pliable—pulled and folded, rolled and spread out again, it gradually surrendered, warming up and finally becoming round and soft like a woman's breast.

Then he picked the little knife up again and scraped the remaining patina off the board. He cut a slice of the pasta and rolled and pulled it into a long white snake that the knife expeditiously cut into little pieces as if it really were a dangerous beast. Then the little pieces, hollowed out with his index finger like long shells, became gnocchi, and their little army, nicely deployed on the board and covered by a towel tent, waited for the pot to boil.

27.

At the agreed-upon hour, the two guests arrived. While the elder brother entered the teacher's abode and offered to help, the other man, curious and suspicious, circled the table outside under the trees which had been set for the occasion, sniffing tenaciously as if to ensure that none of the food was poisoned.

The rose of ham, the bread, the amber wine, and especially the aroma of the sauce emanating from the house reassured him. He sat on the bench in front of the table and yanked a small yellowish cheese as shiny as ivory out of the big pocket inside his jacket. He carefully set it next to the plate of ham, between two pot-bellied towers that were the full wine casks, and looked at everything with the bliss of an art lover contemplating a fine still-life painting. But when his brother emerged from the cottage door, religiously carrying the tureen with the gnocchi like a sacred vessel, with the teacher behind him brandishing the ladle, he jumped up and stood at attention the way he did when he was a soldier and a general would pass by.

28.

At first, as always happens, a mysterious silence accompanied the three men's meal. An uninvited contingent had assembled around them—namely the farmers' cat, kittens, and dog, along with the hens from the house. This company reminded the teacher of another house, another family. And the gnocchi seemed hard to him.

They were a bit hard, but the sauce combined with the plentiful cheese was like the colorful, exquisite dress that made even a mature woman beautiful. And Gesuino—more than the others, in fact—abandoned himself to the sensual delight of downing the gnocchi one after another, first sucking them dry like candies, and as his fork seized one, he was already eyeing the next, until his plate was empty. Then he took a piece of bread to finish cleaning his plate, but the host swiftly and abundantly refilled it.

Gesuino sighed, overcome with happiness, and picked his fork back up with a resigned air to begin the process anew. Now, however, he was aware of what was happening around him, and since the dog was staring at him, wagging his straight tail like an imploring finger, he tossed him one of the gnocchi, but a kitten was quick to grab it for himself.

29.

The other brother ate with greater cunning, hiding his pleasure. His eyes, however, smiled at the flasks, and when the teacher had filled the first two glasses with wine and then poured into his own only water that had neither color nor consistency, those eyes sparkled with both compassion and joy. Compassion for the man who was drinking water, joy for the hope that the flasks would be reserved for the guests alone. But the very bounty of the wine prevailed over his selfishness.

"You aren't drinking?"

"I don't drink. The doctor forbade it."

Those words were received like a cruel bit of news. Even the taciturn Gesuino lifted his fork like a menacing trident.

"Curse doctors and their medicines."

Thus began their conversation.

"Once the doctor ordered me to not drink wine too, and not to eat meat or pasta or beans. My wife, who was a rare gem, didn't say a word to the doctor, but once he'd gone, she told me: 'Proto, you just need to entrust your soul to God.'"

"I remember now!" hollered Gesuino. "And your wife immediately began cooking beans and went to buy wine. The next day you were feeling better."

"Well then, drink, to the doctor's health."

"Another time…"

But it would take too long to report all the mortal dangers avoided by disobeying the doctor which Proto recalled before Gesuino finally recounted a good one.

"Once I sprained my ankle. Proto's wife beat an egg with oil and rubbed it into the joint and then wrapped a tight dressing around it. Three days later, I was healed. I bet that if we'd called the doctor, he would've had to amputate my foot."

The teacher smiled obligingly and then talked about happier things.

They also spoke of ways to combat ants, and how it's necessary to leave beans and peas on the plant until they dry completely when it's the seeds you want. Only towards the end of the meal, when the nice round cheese was cut into wedges and seemed to sweat from the pain but then gladly offered itself to the guests' mouths, did the discussion turn serious again.

It was Gesuino himself who laid out the question: "Why does even the most peaceful man constantly create troubles?"

His face, beneath its crown of red ringlets, had turned a nice orange color, and his little bluish eyes shimmered behind a veil of tears. Since the other two men were looking at him a bit hesitantly, he slapped his palm on the table and nodded toward the main house.

"I mean, why the devil did those people there, who had everything they could possibly want, ruin everything for themselves like that?"

Proto looked at the teacher, winking to apologize for his brother's simple-mindedness, and quickly explained, philosophically, the reason for the tragedy: "Because they were all mad as a hatter."

And then he attacked the second flask of wine by himself.

"Of course… How did the story go?" the teacher asked.

"The story was that they were too well off, father and sons. But the old man held onto the money while the sons wanted to have a good time. That led to constant arguments and fights, until the sons went crazy and killed their father."

"Crazy?" Gesuino reflected, now irked by his brother's explanation. "Wicked is what they were, and God punished them."

"What God? God doesn't meddle in such things. Otherwise, he'd be wicked too."

Gesuino turned purple. "You talk that way because you lack religion."

"Or maybe I'm more religious than you, if only you'd admit it."

One of their usual fights already seemed to be erupting when the teacher intervened:

"The fact remains that man needs to stir, to fret. It starts as soon as he's born. Life is movement, and even the stars and the sea never stand still. God, however, has given man wisdom, and so it's man's duty to put his capacity for action to good use, to work and live in peace with himself and others. Anyone can do it, if he so desires."

"One tries and tries, but doesn't succeed," replied Gesuino. "Besides, it's other people who cause problems."

"Who, me?" said Proto, getting worked up. "But I'm the most even-tempered man in the world."

"I'm not talking about you two," the teacher resumed, pouring them something to drink. "Well, yes, you two as well. You love each other, but you still fight all the time. Let's hear why."

"It's him, it's him!" exclaimed Gesuino, pointing a finger at his brother. "He thinks everything I do is wrong, he criticizes everything, or worse, he ridicules it. In short, he treats me like a little boy or an idiot because he thinks he's better than me. But—"

"But you think you're better than him. Everyone's that way! The fact is that we've forgotten Divine Law. *Humble yourselves before the Lord and he will exalt you.* And we've also forgotten the Ten Commandments. I bet you don't even remember them, Gesuino. Nor you, Proto."

"*I* certainly don't," Proto replied with a faint smile of derision, not directed at himself or the teacher, but at his brother who noticed it and felt his bile continuing to rise. But

145

with some effort, he controlled himself and humbly confessed that he didn't remember the Commandments very well either.

Then the teacher pulled the pipe out of his pocket, and when Proto did likewise, he offered him some tobacco.

Gesuino didn't smoke.

"I have no vices," he said, a bit spitefully. Meanwhile, he slowly drew the flask towards him, and taking advantage of the two men's preoccupation, kept drinking. The teacher, however, saw everything and recalled Marga's claims that Antonio had no vices. While Proto, between one round of spitting and another, continued to philosophize, he smoked tenaciously, looking up at the blue sky, already silvery with the first trace of twilight, and he lost himself there, with sorrow and with joy.

30.

That second night was more peaceful. He no longer felt alone in that gloomy, cursed enclosure, or that he'd wasted his day. The two brothers, after the elder had helped put away the kitchen things, left happy and finally in harmony. Even the dog was wagging his tail and looking at him, and while the kittens played amongst themselves under the table, the cat conducted a silent exploratory tour of the room. It seemed he'd finally created a new family and had high hopes that time would be on his side.

When he woke up early the next morning, he actually felt that something in him, in his flesh and spirit, was already renewing. He jumped nimbly out of bed, filled with courage, no longer afraid of running into his fellow man. And so he decided to go do his shopping himself. He freshened up like when he went for a walk with Ola. He followed *their* path and seemed to hear her silent little footsteps on the grass, cool and crisp in the sea breeze.

But his new suffering was already dissolving into the backdrop of his past suffering, and he was making an effort to believe that Ola had grown, that she was no longer a little girl, that she'd grown and detached from him the way children even gradually detach from their parents.

In the market piazza, the women looked at him like they did the first morning after his arrival. So alone, without Ola, he even seemed like a different man to them. One of them, from whom he occasionally bought some fruit for the girl, asked about her.

"She's out with her mother."

"I see. Ornella hasn't been around for two days either. Where did that pain in the neck go?"

He didn't reply, intent on selecting a bit of fruit. The woman also sold small cheeses like the one Gesuino had brought, and he stocked up on them. Then he went to the baker.

The baker was a friend of Antonio's.

"So he's coming back today, our overgrown boy," he said to the teacher as he weighed the bread that smelled fresh-baked.

"He sent me a postcard, with a beautiful woman on it," he added with a wink.

The teacher took the bread wrapped in tissue paper, and it felt warm, as if alive.

Ah, so Antonio hadn't yet returned. That explained the past two days' peace and quiet. He had some misgivings about having left the house alone, at the mercy of Ornella, but what was done was done. Back in his own abode, he resumed his life. Deep down, though, he was expecting something new, and this waiting began to unsettle him again. By the afternoon, it became agonizing. Perhaps the weather was causing it, since the sky had grown dark and thunder was rising from a turbulent sea. Flash after flash of lightning crossed the sky, as if pushed by the wind, brushing against the windowpanes that seemed to tremble in fear.

Closed up in the room, he felt an undefinable fear as well. His blood was tumultuously pooling around his knees like a crowd in the bend of a too-narrow street, and a distressing foreboding that something terrible was due to happen at any moment took complete hold of him.

A tenuous veil of rain suddenly obscured the air's ominous glow. The wind and the lightning ceased. The motionless trees seemed to offer themselves to the water with zealous delight, and the water stopped there, becoming one with the leaves.

The lightning erupted again, stronger. The rain stopped, as if frightened, and the wind took savage pleasure at shaking the water from the leaves until an eye opened in the sky, in between the trees, spying on what was happening on the earth. Then the sun drove away the oppressive mantle of clouds surrounding it, and the lightning, thunder, and wind all began their own retreat.

Total tranquility returned. The man, however, didn't regain his calm. It was as if the storm had taken refuge inside him.

As evening approached, he took his usual walk around the big house to be sure that everything was as it should be and saw a figure pressed against the bars of the gate, arms spread wide as if nailed to a cross. From the top of the path he couldn't recognize who it was, and yet he immediately sensed that it was her, Ornella. He considered hiding, but she'd apparently been there a long time and was determined to wait an eternity for him. The reddish figure against the void of the colorless background reminded him of *that other one*. Frightened, he approached.

"What do you want?" he asked brusquely.

Her response was, however, calm: "Let me in."

"What do you want?"

He was determined not to let her in. He once again perceived her animal heat and scent, giving him the impression that a noxious beast, a big angry cat feigning calmness in order to slip into his domain, was clinging to the gate, and he recalled Ola's words:

The Mammon cat does exist, I heard it myself!

"I must speak with you," she said, staring at him with her cruel green eyes.

149

"You can talk from there. I'm listening."

"Fine," she exclaimed arrogantly. "It's your own fault if anyone hears me! Your son came home today and when he read your letter, he threw me out. When I refused to leave, he took a whip to me, threatening to kill me. I have the marks here, on my arms and back. And I don't know where to go. Now you must go tell him to provide for me. Or else…"

"Or else?"

"Or else something serious will happen. I'm like a rabid beast, can't you tell? I'm capable of anything. Anything!" she screamed, furiously rattling the gate, and her eyes glimmered like those of a caged tiger.

He thought of Ola. Ornella was capable of taking revenge on her. At that moment he felt he was on his deathbed, on the threshold between the frightening mystery of life, interwoven with mistakes, suffering, and penance, and the even more frightening, inexplicable mystery of the hereafter.

He opened the gate and let the woman in.

That move immediately seemed to if not placate her, at least subdue her. Without another word, she followed him to his room and collapsed, drained of all energy, onto the chair he offered.

In the dim light from the small lamp perched on the table, he observed that her face was distraught and had suddenly aged. Her hair even looked like it had been burned, and on her white neck, the purple and red surface of an ecchymosis revealed the blows she'd received. Knowing that talking is the most effective way for a woman to vent, he asked:

"Tell me what happened."

But Ornella was different from other women. Like lesser beings, she was unable to express pain without screaming. In fact, she lowered her head, bit her arm, and began moaning with savage shrieks, and he truly felt that he was facing a wounded beast. Words were useless. Some other solution to help her had to be found.

"Don't scream, Ornella. What's done is done. He struck you in a moment of rage, but he'll regret it and will certainly provide for you. I'll take it upon myself, to convince him. In the meantime, have something. Do you want to eat? Do you want a bit of wine? There's no use continuing to shriek, Ornella. Everything will work out, you'll see. Meanwhile, tell me," he suggested with a tenuous, falsely humble voice, "do you truly have no one you can go to?"

She had some relatives in town but didn't want to go there. She wanted to return to the nice warm nest she'd been driven from, like a crow banished from a dove's nest. The impossibility of that return exasperated her despair.

Not even the hospitality that he offered for that night, saying that up in the loft was a clean little bed, seemed to calm her. She sobbed at length, shaking her head against her arm, and only when she was tired did she lift her red face and with a rasping voice say:

"Couldn't you go and talk to your son right away?"

"It's too early. Don't you realize that he might still be angry too?"

She hid her face again. Lifting it one more time, she again stared at the schoolteacher with her savage eyes filled with hatred and madness.

"And couldn't you go back to living with them? Only that would mollify him, only that…"

"We'll do that too, if need be," he said nervously and then went outside because he was suffocating. Passing by the window he saw Ornella drinking the wine he'd poured. Maybe that would calm her down. The one who couldn't calm down was him.

He walked around the big house again. He'd never been superstitious and didn't want to be, but he felt like he'd been overwhelmed by the evil influence radiating from that dead, cadaverous house.

His instinct was to run away, far away, where others' evil couldn't catch him. He was already opposing God and his own conscience—what more was expected of him? Hadn't he already given it all?

He went to sit in front of the marble table where he'd eaten with the farmers, and he seemed to hear the echo of his words. As the turmoil in his blood died down, his thoughts and his opinion of himself became clear once again. A bright, cold light like that of the moon prevailed around him, making the shadows of things more vivid than the things themselves. All was tranquil and still now, like in the eternal repose of death.

"I need to surrender to myself as well," he thought. And he decided to keep Ornella with him, to take care of the baby. He would have to fight to do it. Actually, he would have to battle the savage strength of the woman herself, and then take on other trials and tribulations, but the very thought of the fight inspired him.

"Come on, you can do it," he said softly to his shadow. "God will assist us."

Then he stood and walked toward the hedge, thinking he'd heard something. Under the moon everything was peaceful, bathed in a fantastic color that wasn't really a color but wasn't black either. Some leaves shone like gilded glass in the moonlight, others like alabaster.

The farmers' dog began to bark. Gesuino's voice called out, and without knowing why, the teacher called out as well: "Oh, Gesuì?"

Gesuino didn't answer, but he approached the hedge, where a gap closed only by a branch allowed the farmers to communicate with the caretakers of the house. The teacher headed there too, and they were like two explorers in an unknown land who hear each other through a dense wilderness and try to reach one another.

They in fact did meet at the gap. The bare, black branch still separated them, but they could easily see and talk to each other.

Gesuino wasn't wearing his hat. His reddish curls looked like dry grass, and the white of his eyes shone like porcelain.

Behind him stood the dog with his long shadow. Restless, he yelped and chewed on a spot under his thigh, as if he had fleas, and then hearing the voice of his master, he raised his head.

31.

"Is there someone there with you?" Gesuino asked. "The dog was barking at your house."

A moment of silence, and the teacher seemed to hear large wings pass in the solitude of the heavens, reviving dead things. It was the assistance he'd been expecting from God.

"There's a woman with me," he said in a tranquil voice. "An unfortunate soul who doesn't know where to go and came flapping around here like an injured bird."

But the analogy was lost on Gesuino.

"Do you know her?"

"Yes, I know her. She's the servant who used to live with my son Antonio."

Gesuino, who rarely left the farm and didn't get involved in others' business, didn't know Antonio nor his servant, but his innate understanding of sin vaguely revealed their tragic story.

"Does your son have a wife?

"A wife and a daughter."

"But then they threw this servant out? Why?"

The teacher felt he was being interrogated. Fair enough. Man is the judge of man.

"It was actually my son who threw her out because his wife and daughter are away. And he threw her out because she's pregnant."

"Oh, good for them! And you're letting her stay with you?"

"Gesuino," the teacher said then, grabbing onto the hedge, "please don't judge me harshly. You're a man of God and a man of conscience, and so you must help and advise me. What should I do? The girl is desperate. She could harm herself or others. I'm certainly not happy about letting her stay with me; in fact, I'm almost afraid of spending the night with her. What should I do?"

Gesuino grabbed onto the hedge as well, his mind muddled.

"Let's ask Proto. He's a man of the world and might have something to say."

"No, no, you have to tell me, according to your conscience."

"But who's the man who impregnated her?"

"I don't know, and it's not important. What is important is keeping the girl under control so she doesn't do anything stupid, and then helping her find a solution for her little one."

"My brother Proto would say to let her hang herself. First these females have their fun, and then they back someone else into a tight corner."

"That's true, but Jesus even extended a hand to Mary Magdalene. Forget about Proto, Gesuino—give me your advice."

The other man was reluctant to give advice. Instead, he probed further.

"It wouldn't by chance be your son?"

"I don't know. Even supposing it was him, the fact remains that he threw her out of the house, and so I'd be doubly obligated to protect her and to protect the baby."

"That pig…" muttered Gesuino.

The teacher didn't defend Antonio, but said: "People sin without knowing and without trying. It's up to men of conscience to set things straight. When the river floods, what fault does it bear? But men build embankments and the disaster is remedied. That's what we must do."

Gesuino bowed his head in such a way that the moon illuminated his hair like a field of stubble. He was looking at his shadow, hidden in the hedge, as if asking its opinion. There was a period of silence, broken when the dog lifted his head high and barked to alert those near and far that the calm was illusory, that they were vigilant and ready to ward off any attacks. Then his master looked up too and said:

"You are a man of honor. I'm certain my brother Proto will help as well. What should we do?"

"Well, for now, don't let anyone know that the woman is here. It's best to avoid gossip. Also, if you see her, don't mention her condition, don't act surprised in any way. I'm certainly allowed to have a servant, like I've always had. True," he added sarcastically, "we weren't sleeping in the same cottage before, but anyway, it's all the same. Finally, when I have to go out to see to her business and try to set things right, you have to keep an eye on her and pay attention to what's going on around here. Am I asking too much of you?"

"Not at all!" the other man exclaimed, shrugging his shoulders. The surly curmudgeon from before seemed to have returned.

32.

Even the short and sweet June night helped the teacher. After having conferred with the other farmer, who immediately grasped the entire situation without commenting, he doubled back, repeating his tour of the garden and house. Everything was tranquil. Even the marble tables, in the tree-shaded moonlight, and the cool, crisp benches seemed to offer themselves to him, if he wanted to lie down and leave some of his pain behind. But his pain felt like a supporting rod inside him, from his heels to his neck, and he didn't want to surrender it to anyone.

The lamp was still burning in the room. The woman, however, had gone up to the loft to lie down on the bed. Left behind on the floor under the stairs were the dusty red slippers she wore only in the house, the same ones she'd run off in to escape Antonio's fists.

The teacher stared at the slippers, imagining they should move and speak. They did, in fact, reveal to him the violence of the scene that had taken place between the two people: the man's rage must have been savage for Ornella to have run off like that. And yet, he didn't regret that evidence. Perhaps it signified Antonio's rebellion against his own perverted inclinations, and by lashing out at the woman, he'd also struck his own conscience.

Or were those just his own illusions? At any rate, he felt relatively calm. He went to bed, put out the light, and closed his eyes. He felt like he'd walked a long way that day and could finally rest.

Once again the far-off sound of an organ in the crystal temple of the sea appeared, along with a song that illuminated the night:

> *The sailor on the waves*
> *Invokes you, oh Lord…*

Ola was playing in the field, a flower amidst the flowers, with a reed bracelet, and in her smooth, little fist, something she wanted to give to her grandfather.

"Grandfather, close your eyes and open your hand." He opened his hand, then opened his eyes to see if something was really there. A glimmer of moonlight penetrated through the window, landing precisely on the palm of his hand, marking it with a stigma of light. Another illusion? In any event, he immediately shut his eyes again, clenching his fist around that pearl of joy.

33.

Ornella got up before him, at dawn. He heard her moving cautiously, trying not to wake him. Then she silently climbed down the stairs, put her slippers on, and went out, closing the door softly behind her.

This behavior reassured him. He got up as well, and when he opened the window, he saw that she had washed herself at the well and was drying off with the edge of her slip. Her back was to him, and her contours were as always: strong, with a grooved back and arms that stuck out like powerful branches. But that almost aggressively exuberant human body no longer intimidated him. It was in front of him, in his dominion, much like a savage tree facing a pruner.

Sensing his presence, she immediately, instinctually resumed her former bearing. Pretending not to see him, she swept up around the well and went to look in on the hens, acting as if the two of them were still *there*, at the scene of the sin and of the pretense. But when he called her from the door, she hastened back, head bowed, humble and glum.

"Ornella," he said with a paternal voice, "you're better at housework than I am. Make the coffee and clean up a bit in here. Meanwhile, I need to go talk to the farmers, and then I'll head into town. Look, Ornella, here's the coffee, here's the coffee maker."

She followed him meekly. The thought that he might be going to look for Antonio to attempt a reconciliation lent her a sense of hope, and thus kindness. With a glance she took in the entire room and immediately knew what needed to be done. She bent over and picked up the coal with her bare hands, and with those bare hands arranged it in the stove and lit a piece of paper underneath it. In a moment the fire was burning, whereas the teacher, once the embers buried in the ash went out, struggled for a long time before managing to achieve such a miracle.

Even the coffee seemed to make itself, under Ornella's gaze, and he found it excellent. With that fine, aromatic taste in his mouth, he went to the farmers to tell them he was going out. Gesuino was also washing himself at the well, shirtless, his hairy chest glistening with drops of water, while Proto, already at work, was reinforcing the handle of a shovel.

The two brothers were already arguing on account of Ornella. Gesuino was muttering some strong words against her and females in general. Proto, just to irritate him, was voicing anger at the wild young men who seduced them. But the morning air and the long rays of the sun, still low over the sea, dissipated the men's pointless words.

34.

Once more, the teacher walked the path that now felt like the very path of his life. You come, you go, you think you can never turn back, you think you're leaving your entire past behind. And yet, it all begins anew, and you're walking on your own footprints again, followed by or following after your own shadow.

"But now is the time for action, not philosophizing," the teacher told himself. Then he smiled, imagining that his face reflected the azure ridges of the choppy sea. "And where perchance would I be going? To see Antonio? What can Antonio do? What solution could he come up with? The sin is already circumscribed; it's been quarantined, and it's up to me not to let it spread."

And yet, he was going, and Ola's luminous face accompanied him every step of the way like blind Tobias and the angel. More than once he instinctively bent over to collect some leaf or little flower from the golden furrows of the lane. She used to do that, and he pictured himself as a little boy when he would go in search of medicinal herbs along the roadsides of his hometown.

35

One after another, he retraced all the familiar streets. Antonio wasn't at home. The farmer's wife, temporarily taken on as servant as well, eyed him with malice and asked if he'd had a good journey. He didn't reply. Instead, he lingered to pay attention to the dog who was fawning on him and who followed him to the gate, intending to go out with him.

"No, not now, that's a good boy," he said, confiding in the animal better than the woman. "You have to keep watch here while everyone's away. When Ola comes back, I'll come and get you both, okay?"

The dog lowered his ears in a sign of acquiescence, and after the teacher left and shut the gate behind him, he barked at the air to show he was there doing his duty. The man walked away, to continue doing his duty as well, but it felt like he was doing it in a vacuum, like the dog.

He followed the street to the wharf, and then to the fish market. Antonio wasn't there, and he was almost happy not to run into him. Nevertheless, he continued his search. He went back up the entire street along the canal, turned left, and made his way into the heart of town. Antonio wasn't there, but at the corner of the piazza, between the bakery and the wine and spirits shop, where the sidewalk was furnished with tables and chairs and decorated with vases full of greenery, a group of his friends were chatting and watching people go by. The teacher was immediately in their line of sight; he wished he could turn back and hide around the corner, but by that point he felt like he had absolute self-control, including over his every impulse. So he kept walking, greeting those who greeted him, and continued on his way.

The women selling herbs and fruit called out to him. He stopped by the one he usually frequented and bought some cherries, intending to please Ornella. Then he suddenly jumped, startled at the deepest, most mysterious part of his humanity as he realized that a new emotion—not fear, not respect, not pity, but rather love and an almost paternal

162

instinct—was already binding him to the woman, or rather, to the little being inside her.

36.

Then he made the other necessary purchases, and finally, very slowly, walked down the grassy street—*their* street. He sat for a moment on a stone post and pictured Ola beside him, with a pair of shiny cherry earrings amidst her silky black curls. But why did his heart no longer ache with her memory? In fact, that organ song that lifted him up on its wings of light was now becoming the theme music that accompanied her reappearance in his thoughts. He felt like he'd already been reclaimed by God's infinite goodness.

37.

Stepping inside, he immediately noticed that something new had also reinvigorated his abode. A woman's touch, even if only mechanically, had passed over the objects, the walls, the floor. Water had refreshed and cleaned what was dirty, some things so well that they seemed new. The soul of the house, the fire, was burning brightly. Lastly, he noticed that everything in the loft had even been cleaned, a sure sign that Ornella had no intention of leaving.

She was next to the well, leaning over the tub, washing his shirt. Seeing him return, she'd jumped up, her eyes the color of the surrounding leaves. Then she hunched down again, more than before, hiding herself. Now, setting the provisions on the table, he heard her angrily beating the article of clothing against the washboard.

"Harder, harder—you probably need something to beat on," he thought. Then, through the window he said: "Ornella, I brought you cherries. Do you want them?"

She stood up again, fiercely controlling herself. But her lips were trembling, pale with anxiety but with scorn as well.

"Did you at least bring my shoes?" she asked with her savage voice.

The schoolteacher was no longer intimidated.

"What do you need shoes for? You're not going anywhere today anyway. Besides, I didn't find Antonio, at home or in town."

She began ferociously wringing the poor shirt in her hands.

"I knew he'd go into hiding, I knew it! Good-for-nothing coward, son of a bitch…"

A string of obscenities streamed from her mouth, falling into the tub's livid water, and the teacher let her pour all her poison out. Better outside than inside.

38.

Still, the cherries produced a certain effect. After she'd hung the shirt, she came back inside, arms still wet, and seemed immediately drawn to that bundle of great big blood drops.

Slowly, slowly, she took one, looked at it, and put it in her mouth, slowly detaching it from the stem. Then she spat the pit into her palm and held onto it as if not wanting to throw it away.

Suddenly she thought about Ola too, with a savage desire to be reunited with her, to feel the girl's fresh fruit face against her own rage- and pain-parched face, to eat cherries together and play with their stems and pits. Never again. It would never happen again. Her eyes at last grew damp with tears.

She put the cherries on a plate and approached the window to wash them. There she saw two eyes that strangely resembled her own, looking like those of a cat waiting to be tossed something to eat. For a moment they stared at each other, the four green eyes with an animal-like glint of curiosity, and then she laughed and was the same old Ornella again.

Gesuino, outside, seemed dazzled. He'd come to see her, and seeing her like that, with those vivid flesh tones, the yellow of her hair, and the red of the cherries and her dress, fully satiated his curiosity. And then came her laugh, like a noose that took him by the neck, giving him a feeling of suffocation. Still, his face maintained its stern expression.

"Is the teacher here?" he asked to signify that he wasn't there for her.

"Don't you have eyes? He's there, behind the well."

She'd put her hand over the cherries and was draining the water from the plate out the window.

"Are you trying to pour that on me?" he shouted, jumping back. "Is that what you really mean to do?"

"Get out of the way," she hollered insolently, splashing him with the last drops from the plate. He backed up, but kept his eyes locked on hers, and she held his captivated gaze with victorious glee. Cats stare at each that way before their barbaric battle of passion. The teacher noticed and a ray of hope flashed through his soul. What if Gesuino fell in love with Ornella and married her?

But that ray was quickly extinguished. What about the baby? He couldn't give Antonio's child to the farmers like a puppy to raise. Nor could he take a child from his mother. And above all, he mustn't take the brakes off his imagination and allow these kinds of people to play dangerous games.

When he slapped Gesuino on the back, the man lowered his head like a criminal, and the teacher said dryly:

"It seems you like my maid. Be careful, though, because she's a true pagan, while you're a man of God. Besides, remember yesterday evening's little chat..."

Ornella had stepped away from the window too, suddenly tumbling back into the reality of her gloomy situation. Hearing the teacher's words, she believed the farmers already knew all about her, and a sudden wave of shame swept over her, compelling her to hide.

39.

Proto wanted to meet Ornella too, but while Gesuino, almost like a schoolboy, operated from a turbid sensual turmoil which drove him toward the female, Proto harbored a practical inclination, one of a man who already knew the woman well, and beyond carnal satisfaction, wanted her manual labor and possibly her servility.

Calculations still vaguely defined wandered through his brain. Ornella's physical condition, rather than giving him pause, gave him good hope. But he was careful not to go see the teacher, and had forbidden Gesuino from going there at all.

When he returned home from town, though, he realized that Gesuino had gone anyway. Not that Gesuino said anything. Red eyebrows knitted, he was actually more taciturn than ever, and already so hard at work that sweat was dripping down his forehead and through that hedge protecting his eyes, finally dropping to the ground. But that very same exasperated exertion, the way he was uprooting the weeds and turning over the earth around the beets revealed the new zest for life that animated him.

Nevertheless, Proto didn't say a word, and for the first time in a long time, that day they didn't argue. It was like they'd agreed to keep quiet. When the dog stood at attention and pricked his ears toward the teacher's house, they ordered him not to bark, but at the same time they listened, both with a sense of curiosity and expectation heightened by the silence around them and especially by that great June serenity that silenced even the sea and spread the leaves on the vines in such a way that the sun could better slip through to reach the maturing grapes.

Seeing the two brothers at work and certain that each would keep the other in check and that together they would keep an eye on Ornella and the house, the teacher went out again in search of Antonio.

But this time he felt guided almost by a sense of joy. He wanted to ask about Marga and Ola and get Ornella's clothes. He felt like he was a ghost himself, walking in a fantastic place where the vivid colors of the landscape, from the blue of the sky and sea to the emerald green of the trees and fields, were as if frozen in time and would never again have to fade away.

Even in Ola's garden, this spell prevailed, carried by the perfume of dropped rose petals. A purifying breeze had passed through there as well. Or was it all a dream, a reflection of an inner light that bathed the teacher's heart?

40.

Hearing footsteps, Antonio burst out of the kitchen, blushing like a woman caught red-handed doing something bad.

"At last I find you," said the teacher, touching his hat in a sign of greeting. "All day I've been looking for you. How's your wife? And Ola?"

His calmness reassured Antonio.

"They're fine. Ola met other children that she has fun with. She even started giving them school lessons right away, if you can believe that!"

"And Marga?"

"Marga's doing better, too. The day before yesterday she still had her usual onset of fever, but less severe, to the point that she got out of bed in the evening. She's quite nervous, though. Come, sit in here," he invited, going back into the kitchen.

The kitchen was in rather a mess, with vestiges of Ornella still visible: her deep blue apron hanging next to the dishrags, her shoes under the table. The cat recognized the teacher and rubbed up against his legs. Even the dog came running from far away, planting himself in front of the man, staring into his eyes with his ears pricked, listening. Every time Ola's name was said, those ears, supple as pasta, drooped a bit before immediately perking back up. Both animals had lost weight, or at least gone hungry.

Amidst those signs of disorder, Antonio remained, after his initial moment of surprise, seemingly unchanged. He was carefully dressed with a clean shirt and an orange silk tie, nicely knotted. Not only that, but he had brand-new shoes, the same color as his tie, and he explained that his absence that morning was due to those shoes, because he'd had to go to the neighboring city to find ones that suited him.

His sweet, limpid eyes, modestly veiled by long lashes, were the most innocent around, so much so that the teacher was once again moved by them, even though his own benevolence irritated him.

Despite that reaction, he asked with his own unintentional naiveté:

"You're alone here?"

"Yes, all alone. I kicked that trollop out."

"I know," the teacher said, regaining his sense of reality, "and I'm here to ask why."

"You know the reason better than I do. I threw her out because you left."

"And if I hadn't gone, you would still have her here?"

"I don't know. I do know that you left me that derisive letter, and so I lost my head and gave her what she deserved."

"But do you know about her current condition?"

"Oof!" the younger man snorted. "You take things too seriously. She's been a fallen woman since childhood. And she's the one who approaches men, so there's no need to shower her in kindness."

"You, though, Antonio, didn't treat her so badly when it suited you, and like it or lump it, the baby inside her is yours. Let's drop it, anyway. Talking to you is like talking to… I won't say like talking to this dog who's more perceptive that you, but like talking to a wall. Besides, I'm only here to ask you to give me that poor wretch's clothes at least."

"Oh, so she came to you? Did she steal your heart, too? Watch out."

Jealousy, derision, shock, inquisitiveness, and even cruelty resonated in his voice. The teacher was prepared for any attack. In fact, he almost enjoyed it and was having fun with it.

"Oh, yes, I'll be careful. But who knows, maybe I'll end up being the one to marry her? At any rate, since I have little money for her hope chest, I'll ask you again to give me her clothes and shoes."

Antonio glowered, looking at his feet. "Where is she?"

"What do you care?"

"I do care, though. People say one thing but think another."

"She's staying at my place," the teacher replied, his voice firm and sad.

The other suddenly looked up, with the rage and humiliation of a man defeated and mocked.

"So where are you staying?"

"Again, what difference is it to you? If you cared, you would've come to visit me. Instead, you went off to buy new shoes."

Antonio jumped to his feet, clenching his fists as if he wanted to pummel the teacher. He walked to the doorway to catch his breath and then returned to sit down with a rigid posture.

"You're right. Disowned by God, I'm worse than any beast. I've always done things my own way, always prodded by the devil. But now I want to rely on you, the way I should have as a little boy. Tell me what I must do."

"You must promise never to go near that woman again. When the baby is born, we'll take care of him."

"I'll be the one to take care of him," Antonio said wretchedly. "I'll put him in boarding school."

"The minute he's born? They might not accept him."

Was he joking, or was the teacher mocking him now? Antonio looked at him sullenly and then laughed. And his laugh sounded so much like Ola's that the shadow over their conversation turned to light.

41.

Then they agreed upon a course of action, taking everyone into consideration. The farmer's wife was tasked with finding a trustworthy and earnest woman to manage the housework before Marga's return. Then the teacher advised Antonio not to tell his wife anything until the matter was resolved, and to instruct his tenant farmers to remain silent.

He intended to keep Ornella with him. Where this sacrifice would lead, he didn't know, but placed his trust in God. Meanwhile, he unhesitatingly accepted the monthly subsidy Antonio was offering to the woman, given that he was poor and his tiny teacher's pension and the interest from the sum obtained from the sale of his house barely sufficed to live on.

Antonio, on the other hand, was rich. So rich that instead of taking his wallet from the inside jacket pocket the way men who know how much cash they possess customarily do, he pulled a handful of rolled-up banknotes from his pants pocket, a disorderly mix of large and small bills, and when two of them dropped to the ground, he let the teacher bend down to collect them. The teacher accepted those very two bills, folded them one at a time, and thoughtfully and attentively placed them in his worn but intact old wallet, in the compartment where he kept the photograph of Antonio as a little boy and a red, heart-shaped pebble that Ola had found and given him on the seashore.

42.

He personally carried the bundle of Ornella's things, shoes included, home. His gait was heavier on that trip back, not due to the weight of the burden, but due to the weight of his thoughts.

"When she sees that she's been unequivocally rejected, God knows what kind of scene she'll make," he thought. He cautiously opened the gate for which he possessed the only key, and proceeded almost timidly, setting the bundle down in a corner behind the house. He wanted to investigate Ornella's mood first. But no matter how hard he looked, he didn't see Ornella in the cottage or outside. Through the wide-open door he could see the chickens running amok inside. Two young cocks, yellow and brown, as prickly as raw lobsters, were ferociously pecking at each other under the table, and the fiery rooster and a young pullet as white as a dove were making themselves right at home.

"Good job, good job!" he said, clapping his hands as if applauding them.

And once he'd managed to chase out even the two combatants who were blind and deaf to anything except their animosity, he went to the farmers' place to look. That's precisely where Ornella was, in the fine, placid sunshine, her tall figure dominating the green and blue backdrop, her braided circle of tresses appearing to touch the sky. The two brothers were staring at her, tiny behind her, still a bit stooped in their labor, leaning slightly toward her. All three were laughing and talking in a vulgar way, enthralled by the same savage spell. And he lost all hope for God's mercy.

43.

This state of things lasted several weeks, worsening in fact with the arrival of hot weather.

Day by day, the teacher felt his misery spreading over him. He tried in vain to free himself from it—can one free oneself from the nightmare of the heat? He needed to run away, climb to the summit of the mountains or to the high horizon of the sea where the atmosphere was pure. But he couldn't move. He couldn't and didn't want to, since he knew that even escaping to a cooler place wouldn't bring relief. And so he accepted his punishment the way he accepted the shallow, resolute heat of that plain where everything was burning, like in his soul, and where the healthy sea air was unable to consume the baleful air of the rice paddies and salt mines.

Even Ornella seemed resigned. She would go buy groceries and work in the vegetable garden, taking advantage of the farmers' proximity to laugh or bicker with them. And those two had also begun fighting again, ostensibly for other reasons, but really because of her. Gesuino was going to Mass every morning now, to have an excuse to run into her when she left to do the shopping, but also because he was tormented by doubt and wanted to extinguish his diabolic passion with prayer and religious observances.

One evening when he was alone in the cottage, the teacher heard Proto, with an unctuous voice, asking permission to enter.

"Come in," he said, immediately sensing that something was new. He carefully folded the newspaper he was reading and removed his little reading glasses, carefully putting them back in their black case.

"What's this?" Proto asked with a false voice. "Your woman isn't home yet?"

"So it seems. She went to buy milk in town."

"And you allow her to stay out so late?"

"What can I do about it? That's how it is."

Proto turned serious, almost sad.

"That's how it is," he sighed. "Women are all the same. Gesuino swears that not a single one is honest. Truth be told, my wife was; that much I can personally vouch for. In her youth, she really loved having fun too. But I'm of the opinion that a good husband makes a good wife—especially with the help of a cudgel. One time a friend of mine—"

The teacher didn't seem inclined to listen to the illustrative examples that Proto always used to support his opinions, and so he looked him directly in the eye and said:

"Proto, do you have something to tell me?"

44.

Proto realized that with this particular man, he needed to cut out the chit-chat and get right to the cold, hard facts.

"The fact is this," he said, tensing up. "Perhaps you've guessed. That girl is well suited for me. She's healthy and robust, and with me, along with Gesuino's supervision, she'd toe the line."

"What if Gesuino is more infatuated with her than you are?"

"It doesn't matter. He'll get over it, and if not, I'll make him get over it. I'll send him away, that's all, have him lead his own life. But that won't happen because we love each other too much. You're familiar with the proverb: *Where you eat is where you complain.*"

"The girl is five months pregnant, you know that, and she's even already showing."

"It doesn't matter. We'll wait until she gives birth, breastfeeds, until everything falls into place. The child—oh, of course I'll take him, I'll legitimize him."

The teacher was left shaken in the face of this rock-solid serenity. It all seemed like a natural phenomenon to him, and he wondered if he—he alone—wasn't the one standing outside human normality. But deep down he felt that wasn't true, and instead of being happy for that return of God's mercy calming the agitated waves around him and guiding his boat to shore, sadness grew in the roots of his soul.

"Does the girl know anything about this?"

"Well, to be honest, I hinted at it. She didn't respond, but I noticed that she took a good look at the house, the livestock, and the field, appraising everything and examining what there is and what it could yield. She's a practical girl, and I like that too. She's efficient with the housework—more than most girls I know. Am I right?"

"You're right," the teacher confirmed, looking around, and the farmer's gaze followed his. The dwelling did in fact seem transformed, with the bed clean, the radiant scene of the *Flight*, the oil-polished chest of drawers, and all the orderly things on top. On the hood of the stove hung a green paper doily. The floor was clear of everything that wasn't furniture feet, and on the back wall, the cooking utensils looked like decorative studs.

Meanwhile, the alarm clock ticking away atop the chest of drawers showed a quarter to nine, and she was nowhere to be seen.

45.

"It's this," Proto said, slightly worried. "She's too fond of running around and spending time with men. But it's a malady common to all women, and it passes. Unless…"

There was a dismal pause, and in its silence, the ticking of the clock sounded like the cry of a cuckoo in the desert. The man didn't continue. The teacher didn't ask. Both felt a sense of danger.

At last, Proto, who usually looked his interlocutor in the eye when he spoke, lowered his head and finished his sentence:

"...the girl is still having relations with *that person* you know, and you need to intervene and put a stop to it."

The teacher didn't bat an eye. He recalled Ola's game when she would jump on his shoulders and say "Let's see who can keep their eyes open longer" while assaulting his face with the breath from her laughing mouth. And that memory sustained him yet again in that moment of danger.

46.

"Who told you that Ornella is still having relations with Antonio?" he asked firmly.

Proto looked up, almost surprised that the teacher knew that *that person* whose name had never been spoken between them was in fact Antonio.

"I saw it myself. First I saw them confabulating in the boulevard, and then I tailed her and saw her going into his house. Gesuino can confirm all this as well."

The teacher automatically put his glasses back on like he did when he wanted to see something clearly up close, and then took them off again, holding them as he gestured, his hand trembling with indignation.

"And you want to marry a woman like that? You, Gesuino, and her… in a fine pigsty…"

He stopped himself, but too late. Proto was offended. More dignified than the teacher, though, he said:

"My house has always been clean. Humble but clean. And I guarantee you that it will remain clean whether that woman— or any other—comes into it."

"Even if she betrays God?"

"God is one thing, I'm quite another," Proto declared without a trace of irony. The teacher, who at times had the grandiose assumption of believing that he himself was a part of God, truly felt infinitely different from the farmer.

In any event, he asked for time to reflect.

47.

In early September Marga returned. Her health was much improved: the fever had become intermittent, increasingly subdued and brief, assailing her only in the afternoon and vanishing with the setting sun. Since the teacher never appeared, not even to collect the monthly allowance agreed upon with Antonio, one day she and the little girl went looking for him in his refuge. By then everyone knew that he was living down there with Ornella, whom it was said was pregnant because of him. People whispered and laughed, but without surprise or contempt. Those things happened in the world. He wasn't even offended anymore. His old sorrow had returned, an inseparable companion, but he was consoled by a

179

secret hope for better days. Something was bound to happen, be it even his death, to put an end to the sad sequence of events overwhelming him. And he waited, like a leaf on a tree that one day would have to escape the wind and sun and fall back into the bosom of the earth.

Meanwhile, he was in fact living amidst the trees and bushes of his garden, deluding himself that he was working the soil. In reality, he was seeking out a final comfort by blending in—or trying to blend in—with nature.

And he seemed to be happy when she was in step with him, when the peach tree tossed its mature fruit at his feet, when the insects grew familiar with his hair and clothing, when the green spider ran across his hand like it was a leaf, and when the blood drop that was a ladybug landed on his finger, brown with soil.

Illusions. His heart, inside, was lonely, and his ephemeral joy flew off like the ladybug did after arriving at the very tip of his fingernail.

48.

Only a soul that's suffering in silence can comfort a soul that's suffering in silence. And Marga's visit, even more than Ola's, lifted him up from his sepulchral bowing toward the earth. She feigned nonchalance. She greeted Ornella simply as a former servant who'd taken another position, and let Ola be the one to give her a big hug.

"Goodness, what strength! And how heavy you are, Ola! And how you've grown!"

She'd definitely grown, and some recent scabs and scratches on her velvet arms revealed her latest bouts with the mountain children.

Her meeting with her grandfather was something like that of two lovers seeing each other again after a long absence. Something extraneous had already come between them, and she especially had forgotten and betrayed him. She let him kiss and coddle her, but slipped out of his grasp the way she did on their first meeting. Moreover, she no longer watched him. She already knew him and saw nothing different now, especially since he was wearing the same clothes and the same tie as the last time.

Instead, it was the place that drew her attention, the mysterious place she'd finally penetrated. She took it all in with a glance: the trees, the tables, the well. She maneuvered until she could slip into the cottage. She immediately saw the stairs leading to the loft, and her eyes lit up with savage joy. Up there was mystery, the scent of the old woman who stole children—maybe one was even still hidden up there…

And as she climbed the steps, under the watchful eye of Ornella who seemed interested in nothing else, the teacher and Marga sat outside, in front of the marble table. He was calm as well, almost cold. He looked the woman directly in the eyes and told her that she looked rejuvenated. Then he asked about Antonio and how the household chores were going.

"Oh, good!" she exclaimed. "Antonio surprised me by bringing a new servant into our home, and then he told me that he'd fired this one, who knows why. But the one we have now is pretty good too, and besides, I'm doing better and manage most everything myself. If I recover completely, I can even do without her altogether."

He didn't stop looking at her. And that fine, pale face, her limpid eyes, her pure, girlish mouth, and especially her voice, tenuous and dreamlike, aroused in him a sense of deep admiration all over again. He felt like he was facing a talking statue and wondered why she spoke that way. So that Ornella wouldn't hear? Or was it really because that fine, fickle Antonio, that accomplished imposter, was able to hide the truth from her?

But recalling their conversation after his arrival, he sensed the same atmosphere engulfing them still, and it wasn't his place to cast a shadow on it.

"I want to show you the garden. Come," he said, standing. She followed, docile. She admired the chickens and the brooding hen with her big clutch of yellow chicks, mostly tended by Ornella, actually. She admired the abundant grapes of the pergola and asked about the farmers and the tragic owners of the house.

"The trial will be held before long, and the fugitive will be condemned *in absentia*. The other day an agent came here to establish that everything was in order." Looking at the house and then her, he continued, louder: "Everything is in order when it's closed up and death reigns. That's how it is, Marga."

Marga didn't reply. Only later, when they were down near the hedge, did she say as if she'd thought about it carefully:

"And when you have to surrender guardianship, we hope you'll come back to us. When will that be? Maybe in October?"

"I don't know. The future is in God's hands," he answered, inadvertently imitating the way she spoke.

49.

Days later it was Ornella who asked why he wasn't paying Marga a return visit. The question surprised him at first, but then he pondered what might lie hidden beneath it. Ornella didn't usually speak, panting softly as if her breath had been doubled by that of her baby. She worked in silence, always finding something to do. He watched her from behind, like before. He felt he was seeing her grow, truly swollen by pregnancy, and although she again aroused an instinctual repugnance and dread in him, he watched her with a sense, often deliberate, of reverence. After all, it was the eternal mystery of life ripening within her, and when a tree blooms, you don't look at the ground below, but the sky above.

Her question concealed a certain pitfall, but he felt tired and didn't want to scrutinize anything anymore.

After Marga's visit, the solitude began sucking him dry again, the way a tortoise sucks life from the earth. It purified him, of course, removing obscure particles from his blood, but he felt that when the sucking reached his heart, he would die.

Because it isn't true that a superior man can live alone with nature and inferior beings—his heart needs hearts like own, just the way a column needs others like itself to support a temple.

So one day he went back to see Ola. Ola was sitting under the pergola, barefoot, with a short green dress that made her look like one of those birds that take on the color of the tropical forests where they live. She was playing with the little cat, teasing him with her foot, and after the animal had bounced around her, protruding and retracting his claws, she pressed her bare foot against his belly. But they weren't hurting each other; both were unperturbed in their enjoyment of the seemingly cruel game.

A red butterfly was fluttering around them. It would sometimes approach the kitten's paw, as if overcome by a desire to meddle in their battle, but then immediately change its mind and fly far away. And the leaves were murmuring with a harmonious fluttering that seemed the result of that selfsame murmur.

The teacher approached softly to not spoil the scene, but as soon as his shadow reached the edge of the pergola, the cat ran off and Ola sat there looking at her foot. In fact, she raised it and rested it on her opposite knee, turning it about with her hand to examine it closely.

"Did he scratch you?" the grandfather asked. "Serves you right. You shouldn't be playing games like that."

Ola looked up, and through her wild hair, he saw her eyes turn red and glisten, like two campfires in the woods at night. Then she turned to the wall and began to cry, overcome with desperation and fear. He took her, turned her towards him, and consoled her, remorseful and more distressed than she was. When the storm of sobbing and tears began to subside, he even apologized.

"I wasn't trying to be mean when I scolded you."

"That's not it," she said, calming down. "It's because I thought he'd really scratched me."

50.

Some mornings they still went for a walk along the seashore with the faithful dog. Bathers had deserted the beach, but evidence of their desecration remained, and the little dunes had to be steered clear of because they were filthy with excrement and soiled paper.

"The winter needs to sweep through with its windy broom and its long-range watering can to purify the place," he said to Ola, and Ola laughed at that image of winter as the good Lord's garbage man and asked her grandfather to repeat the sentence.

He repeated it for her, thinking about his adventures, and it seemed to him that the entire throng of middle-class people and farmers that had filled the sea and the sand with their unhealthy sweat had swept over him, just like the legions of pain invoked by God.

"But then there's the snow too," Ola noted, deep in thought. "I don't like the snow because you can't go outside."

"And what if you could go outside?"

"Oh, well then, yes, but they don't want to."

"Then let it snow. It'll purify things better and even kill the fleas, so the dog will be happy."

She laughed again, because the dog proved her grandfather's point by lifting his leg and biting his groin with a howl of annoyance and pain.

"See? Now he has to bite himself to try to eat the fleas."

She laughed. Anything could make her laugh, while he heard a horrible meaning in every single word he uttered.

51.

Then with the rebirth of the grass and the reeds springing up on the dunes, after the northwest wind they called the *garbino* had given the beach an initial cleansing with its formidable broom, the flower of hope was reborn in him as well.

Ornella was becoming larger and more taciturn with each passing day, and he saw something new in her, a pensive reflection in her eyes that were growing paler, allowing him to peer deep inside, as if they were limpid water. And deep inside, a luminous reawakening sparkled. She no longer wanted to leave the house. She didn't even visit the farmers, and the farmers didn't approach unless invited by the teacher. Proto's question, left unanswered, kept everyone anxious. But everyone was waiting for time to resolve matters, as if Ornella's childbirth would mark the beginning of a new life. But what most gave the teacher hope was that sense of conscience that he thought he saw arising in her. Was her maternity the cause? Even animals feel it though, and he didn't want to delude himself too much.

52

Whatever change was taking place in her was also demonstrated by her sudden frugality. Before, she would squander her earnings, legitimate or otherwise, but now she wasn't spending a cent, and she kept her money hidden in the loft.

At the end of each month, Antonio, who also avoided seeing the teacher, would send the established monthly allowance via registered letter. The hundred-lire banknote, marked with little holes from having been stapled to the envelope, passed directly into her hands, and she put it in her pocket without looking at it, and it was never seen again. She was receiving the money as recompense for working for the teacher, but she knew where it was coming from, and in reality, the real boss was her. He was doing the marketing now, and she would complain if he didn't do it right. The women at the market would ask him about her as if she were his wife, and Antonio's friends, always planted at the corner of the piazza, would snicker when they saw him pass by. He no longer took offense, but he felt like a tightrope walker who, despite incredible skill, could plummet at any moment.

He was happy when the winter vented its furious rage against the earth. Between the fog, the wind, and the never-ending rain, he had fewer opportunities to run into his fellow man and be judged by them.

53.

One day he returned home drenched from the rain. The wind had carried his hat away, and he felt like he'd gone bald. Ornella was kind and attentive to him. She made him change his clothes, she took off his shoes, and she had him drink a cup of hot milk. And then she got soaking wet herself going out to fetch wood to stoke the fire.

He sat next to the fire and felt like a little boy again, when his mother would take care of him and make him stay inside on days when the weather was ugly. A pleasant grogginess, like drunkenness, swept his thoughts away. It's nice having a woman in the house, after all, one who saw to the material side of life and let you live the way you wanted. And this Ornella...

"Ornella," he called out, turning to see what she was doing. She was doing the usual—hanging his clothes to dry, and then standing at the table, under the murky light from the rain-pummeled window, peeling potatoes for the soup. And she was doing it carefully, so that the peel came away thin, all in one piece, twisted like a yellow and brown ribbon.

"Ornella, I had a funny dream last night. I thought a bailiff had come to notify me that my guardianship of the house was over. The patricide trial was done, and the authorities were confiscating the convicted sons' property to pay the court costs. But here's the funny thing: the notification letter came from my hometown, and it was from the person to whom I sold my house, and it required me to buy the house back or face its confiscation."

Ornella wasn't accustomed to such revelations from him and didn't understand that he often recounted supposed dreams as a way of revealing his true desires. Nevertheless, she took an interest and made a serious observation, as if it were a real event:

"What did it matter to you if the house was confiscated?"

"That's the point. It shouldn't have mattered to me, but still I felt a profound anguish. And the bailiff dug his heels in and had no intention of leaving until I'd declared my decision. He was a tall man, with a beard, and although he was playing the role of the bailiff, as happens in dreams, he was one of the sons who killed his father, the fugitive one. He sat there, behind the door, and wouldn't budge. I was looking at the letter and thinking of a way to resolve the matter. I thought that Marga would be able to help me…"

Hearing Marga's name, Ornella bowed her head, taking a good look at the potato she was holding, and with a soft voice asked:

"But the money you got from the sale of your house, what did you do with that?"

He didn't reply. That was a matter that had nothing to do with the dream. And besides, at that moment the racket from the wind and rain echoed so loudly that he might not have heard her words.

"Marga will be able to help me," he continued, turning towards the fireplace. "And then things will work out. I'll repurchase the house and go back down there. Down there I can start over and earn money. I can give lessons and open a private school. Everyone respects me down there, and maybe I made a mistake leaving. The house is nice enough, sunny. It doesn't have a vegetable garden or a courtyard, but it's a bit out of the way and looks down on the country road, over a green hill with big olive trees that disappears into the valley below. And above the house and town is the mountain, with its Turkey oak woods and a forest where only hunters dare venture.

Ornella had raised her head. The red veil of the fire's glow flickered like a winter sunset in the gray room. Outside, the storm's frantic tune accompanied the teacher's nostalgic account, and she felt like she was listening to a fairy tale.

54.

It was the beginning of a sort of seduction. Like a serpent drawn to the sound of the flute of a savage who wants to catch it, she drew nearer the teacher as she listened to his stories of that far-off land.

She was especially interested in the hunters who, in summer and winter alike, would make their way into the forest and track down semi-ferocious beasts like the boar and wolf, not without some peril of becoming prey themselves.

"I bet there were werewolves too, the ones that change into men," she said once, and the teacher recalled that Ola also believed in the existence of these mysterious animals that primitive mentalities still used to explain man's savagery.

"It's man who often changes into a wolf," he explained, not without irony, but she didn't even begin to understand certain things and would always superimpose reality over the symbolic.

"But how do they transform? I find these things hard to believe."

And yet, she was afraid of the dead and also claimed to hear strange sounds in the cursed house. One evening when someone came and knocked on the door, she didn't want to answer because—drawing near the teacher in fright to whisper—it had to be the ghost of the father murdered by his sons.

"It's got to be Proto or Gesuino—no one else can enter the property," he said, annoyed.

In any case, he couldn't answer the door because he'd already gone to bed and was sweating. Ever since the day of the big rainstorm, a slight fever and rheumatic pain had been tormenting him.

After knocking on the door, the person outside began tapping, hesitant but persistent, on the window panes.

Ornella screwed up her courage and asked in a booming voice: "Who is it?"

The teacher didn't blame her for not wanting to open the door when an unfamiliar voice replied: "Friends."

"Friends, who?" he shouted then, pulling his head out from under the covers.

The man outside hesitated, then responded in a loud voice as well: "I'm Adelmo Bianchi."

And everything, for a moment, fell silent. Even the trees had stopped rustling. It was one of those dark moments like a pivotal interlude between one act and the next in a great tragedy.

Adelmo Bianchi was the parricide, the father-killer.

"Open the door," the teacher said to Ornella. Since she was frozen in place, face white with fear, he began to get up.

The voice outside resumed: "If it's a bother, don't open the door. I just came to see the house because I'm leaving in an hour, never to return again."

It was one of those passionate voices, gentle and warm, like you only hear on stage. Ornella's terror melted away, becoming a shudder of indefinable emotion, as if that voice were caressing her completely, desperately.

Even the teacher, despite his self-control, felt increasingly sweaty and cold, not because he was afraid of the killer, but because he was dreading all the problems that this visit could entail. Still, he repeated:

"Open the door."

Ornella opened the door, hiding behind it until the frightening visitor was in the middle of the room, and then she softly closed it and looked at his back, disappointed and almost indignant.

He was tiny young man, skinny, poorly dressed. He looked like a vagrant youth, complete with a bag, since he had an old military knapsack. He even had a soldier's beret on his head, which he removed to greet the teacher.

Ornella was following him now, taller than he by a full head, thinking that if he were to lift a finger to hurt anyone, she could crush him in her arms.

For his part, the teacher was thinking of a hoax, of some cruel trick on the part of Antonio's friends, but even though his mind was clouded by his malaise, he didn't allow himself to be overcome by either agitation or anger.

But when the young man was in front of him, respectful and humble, and he could clearly see his face, he no longer had any doubt. It was as if his face had been carved in dark wood and gnawed on by woodworms. The mouth encircled by peach fuzz, the large eyes, and all his features were marked by deep, black creases. It was the very face of retribution itself.

55.

"I'm in bed already because I'm not feeling very well," the teacher said by way of apology. "Ornella, bring a chair over here."

The young man turned to see this Ornella and blushed at finding her practically on top of him, beautiful and gigantic.

"Is this your wife?" he asked stupidly, and then his eyes widened because she was laughing—that vulgar, complaisant laugh she once used to respond to men's complements and rude remarks.

"This is my female companion," said the teacher, overcome as well by an unusual and mischievous joviality. "Sit."

The young man sat, putting his sack on the floor along with his beret, never taking his eyes off Ornella, who was leaning on the foot of the bed as if to protect her employer from any possible peril.

But her presence annoyed the teacher. "Prepare a glass of hot wine," he told her. Then, turning to the young man, "Or do you need something to eat? Don't be shy."

"Thank you, thank you, but I don't want anything. I only came to see the house. I finally have a passport and want to go far away, to the most obscure lands on earth. That way it'll feel like I've gotten my life back. And maybe I'll even make my fortune."

"Perhaps," the teacher acknowledged, "but wouldn't it be better, for your brother's sake as well, to turn yourself in?"

"Turn myself in? Why would I do that? To be sentenced to life in prison? How would that benefit my brother? I'll be able to help him another way, and better, by remaining free." He bitterly added: "If you can call it freedom, living in faraway lands, among strangers, without friends or family or acquaintances. My body will be free, but my soul will forever be a prisoner in this world and the next."

"Then why go?"

"Then why live at all? You go and go, driven by destiny, like sand in the wind. When I lived here, it feels like a hundred years ago, I used to play the ocarina, and one of the little tunes I knew went like this:

> *Like sand in the wind,*
> *Destiny blows us along…*"

And to lend weight to his words, he began whistling the melody.

Ornella, who was preparing the hot wine, turned to look at him. She wanted to laugh some more, but the strange individual's voice enchanted her heart once again. It seemed everything he said was a song. Even the teacher was becoming interested and curious, even though the young man's eyes, with the big, fixed pupils and opaque irises surrounded by too much white, revealed his madness. And he recalled Proto's words: *Madness is the motive behind many crimes.*

"Where have you been all this time?"

"I don't even know myself. Everything is all muddled in my head. First I was down in Sardinia, around Isola Rossa, in a kind of sea cave that few know of. For three days and three nights I didn't eat a thing. Bats were fluttering around me like flies in the dark, and I was terrified of them until I became so angry that I grabbed one and it felt soft and warm in my hand like a frightened little mouse. Then I made friends with them. They seemed just like the thoughts in my head: black, troubled, sleepless."

"You went to school?" interrupted the teacher, surprised as well by the young man's literary imagery.

"Of course. That's what got us into our mess, my brother and I. We went to school all the way to fifth grade—we were in the same class, although he's two years older than me. After that, we had to quit. Our mother, who supported us, had died. He—my father—after that misfortune, became cantankerous, stingy, and spiteful. He forced us to work the land. My brother ran away from home, but later returned, and that's when the fights began, with my father beating him. One morning he beat him with a cane while he was sleeping. The screaming and crying as he awoke are still in my head, in my blood. Why, why, oh Lord, do you allow such horrors?"

He pressed his hands over his ears and closed his eyes, as if still hearing his brother's savage laments. Then he dropped his arms and rested his chin on his chest.

"Many times," he resumed, as if talking to himself, "I find myself conversing with God, and I ask him to explain my crime. I was good. I couldn't even harm an insect. I'd let ants ruin the sown field instead of killing them because I was and am convinced that even animals have a soul and a right to live. Otherwise, how would you explain God and the creation of the world? But this God, this God who created us all to make us suffer? Who constantly drowns us in evil?"

"God is in us, and it lies within us to overcome evil," the teacher said.

Keeping his head lowered, the young man lifted his gaze, and the whites of his eyes shone like porcelain.

"Words!" he exclaimed. "They're easy to pronounce but difficult to put into practice. I used to think like that too, as a boy, when I went to school and read nice, flowery anthologies. But then later…"

"It's never too late to overcome Satan. And perhaps God favors men who give into evil just one time, by allowing them to rise up higher than other men and live solely for the pursuit of what's good and right. Don't you feel like you're one of those men?"

"I do, and that's precisely why I don't want to go to prison. I want to live, work, do good deeds. But too often I'm overcome with despair. I'm alone and cursed. I'll never know love again, never be with anyone again. Even if I were to meet a woman who loved me, I couldn't have her because my father's ghost would come between me and her, and my son would atone for my crime."

"Superstitious nonsense, my son," said the teacher with a compassionate tone. "As long as you think like that, you'll be subject to the Spirit of Evil, and it's he, not the shadow of your father, who clouds your soul. Down there, in the place you talk about going, and where I hope you will arrive soon and safely, no one knows your past. Erase it from your own heart as well, and you'll have a fresh start in life."

"No, no, on the contrary! I want to remember my sorrow and take nourishment from it. And if I meet a woman who wants to share my destiny, I'll tell her who I am, and let her take me as I am, just as I would take her, even if she's more wretched than I am. But let's put the future aside. In the meantime, I'll have to work for my brother as well. If only he'd remained free too! Together it would have seemed we were still happy and that we still could have redeemed our father's life. Sometimes it all seems like a dream to me, and I try to wake up but can't. Even now I feel like I'm dreaming. That's the wall of our house. Inside, everything is just as it was before: our mother is still working for us, my brother is doing his Latin homework, and I'm playing the ocarina. Do you hear it? Do you hear it?"

The only sound was the rustling of the wind, over the roof, but it truly seemed that familial spirits had gathered in the night around the house they used to love long ago.

Holding the cup of hot wine, Ornella listened in bewilderment. Her enormous shadow filled the wall, her head seemingly trying to poke through the ceiling to see the murmuring spirits outside.

56.

Having drunk the wine, the young man first seemed to droop, as if overcome by an invincible drowsiness. Then his face flushed, and his long, feminine hands that were squeezing the cup to warm themselves turned pink, and even his voice grew warmer and more modulated.

"What scares me most is the cold; I can't tolerate it. I wish I could spend the winter sleeping underground like the moles. The heat, though, is my element. That's why I'm going to a sunny country like Australia or one in South America. I want to live like a serpent, in the sun, or in the forests where the leaves are so big that a man can lie down in one like a cradle, and the hollowed-out tree trunks serve as huts. Fishing and hunting to survive, finding myself naked, in touch with virgin nature—that would be my dream come true. But I still have to work, for my brother, and perhaps fortune will instead lead me to the big industrial cities, to the infernal hell-pits where sweat and hard work produce gold. Enough of that. God will help me. If you don't mind, I'll send you my news, and if you could be so kind, you could send me news from here," he said, and then looked around. His wide eyes landed on Ornella again, and since she was staring in fascination at him, their eyes met and desperately locked on one another's as if they were lovers.

The teacher noticed everything and it irritated him. Here that tramp was, getting her claws into someone only passing by for an hour, the last of the scoundrels who another hour from now would be forever blown away by the winds of fate.

He had the feeling he was dreaming as well. His heart was racing, and the heat and the buzzing in his ears indicated a fever. The young man's chatter seemed increasingly incoherent and tedious. He closed his eyes to demonstrate his weariness, but the other man turned around in his chair to face Ornella and continued talking.

"I believe I danced with you once, two or three years ago, at the New Year's Eve ball. I remember because you were already this tall, but not this *fat*, and I was even shorter then. How old do you think I am? I'm not even nineteen yet, but it already feels like I'm a hundred. To top it all off, next year they'll declare me a deserter, even though my dream as a boy was to study and pursue a military career and nobly serve my country. God has other plans, but it doesn't matter. Down there where I want go, maybe I'll also be able to enlist in the colonial militia, and since I have no lack of courage, I'll even be able to distinguish myself and become an officer. Have you ever seen a colonial militia officer?"

She'd never seen one, but immediately pictured him dressed in red and gold, with the greenish plumes of our army sharpshooters, weapons gleaming in the tropical sun. And she didn't answer, partly so the teacher wouldn't hear, but inch by inch, step by step, she approached the young man, as if he were pulling her along by an invisible string, and the more she approached, the more he seemed to recognize her.

"It really was you that I danced with at that ball, two years ago. You were dressed in green, with two of your girlfriends and a masked man. Am I right? Who was he?"

Ornella shrugged. She was sure she hadn't been to the ball two years ago. In fact, she remembered that Antonio had forbidden her from going. But she liked that the young man thought he'd really danced with her.

"It was the last ball I ever went to. In fact, I remember that very night, leaving the party, I got a bronchitis that deteriorated into dry otitis and then into meningitis. For three months I was on death's doorstep and was never the same again. Everything got on my nerves, and the constant fighting between my father and brother made me feel like I'd died and been condemned to hell. If I could write down the dreams I had then, the book would be frightening, more frightening than the *Divine Comedy*. And I have these dreams still. I always seem to be walking either in the desert or in shifting sands where living creatures are tormented by wind that's constantly transforming them, or else I'm in the sea where the waves play the same game, but the beings are happier, albeit a cruel happiness, or else I'm climbing up, up a staircase of boulders, where birds and snakes emerge from the crevices, and then at a certain moment I find myself wedged in between two rocks, with my head over a bottomless abyss. They're the dreams of an overwrought mind, I know, but still they make me suffer terribly. I don't avoid them, though. In fact, I almost love them because to suffer is to atone, and I want to atone. I want to suffer until the pain purifies my blood and my flesh and restores me, like an innocent baby."

He turned back to the teacher, as if to escape the temptation of the woman and continued: "That's why I don't want to go to prison. In prison I'll settle down and become like the others, calm in their punishment, souls already dead. I want to live. I'll go out into the world not in search of freedom, but in search of pain. I'm not, as it might seem, a madman, just a man. I'm a man passing through life like a cloud across the sky. I come from the storm; I'll return to the storm. And if the cloud casts down hail that ruins the harvest and kills the birds, what blame does it take? Likewise, I killed my father because destiny was driving me. If I wanted to turn myself in, I would find a lawyer who could even get me acquitted by showing that I was mentally ill when I committed the crime. But I don't want to. I want to complete my cycle by following my destiny. If they catch me, it means that's how it must be. But they won't catch me. These last few months, I've lived like a wild beast, underground, amidst rocks and bushes, and I've nourished myself with herbs and fruit. I'm no longer familiar with the taste of bread, and the wine that this woman gave me has ignited my head, and I feel like I've talked quite a lot. I swear that I won't drink another drop of wine."

Then he looked at the alarm clock atop the chest of drawers. White and impassive as the moon, its hands continued turning. In the silence, the teacher reopened his eyes and saw that Ornella had returned to the foot of the bed, but with her head lowered, mortified.

"Five more minutes," the young man continued, still looking at the clock. "To tell the truth, I came here with bad intentions. I knew that the caretaker of the house was

202

a weak man, unarmed, and there wasn't even a dog. I came here with the thought of getting into the house at all costs. At all costs, do you understand? I wanted to see our home again and take something from it, at least the ocarina and my mother's wedding ring. They say that your mother's wedding ring brings luck. I had wanted to grab it before the deed, but Heaven help you if you touch a thing in that house. That's where the horrible fights started between us. It means I'll do without it now too. I'll take away a bit of soil on the soles of my shoes!"

And he finally smiled—a smile that carved two dimples in his cheeks and surrounded his eyes with wrinkles, but still made him look young and handsome. It promptly vanished, though, as if he'd lifted his mask of tragedy for only a brief moment to show his true, youthful face.

"If there's something here that you'd like," the master said then, "go ahead and take it."

The young man looked around, as if really choosing an object. His eyes landed on Ornella again, and again his smile appeared and disappeared.

"I'll take this girl along, with her baggage and everything."

She dropped her head even more, mortally wounded by those last words. Nor did the teacher respond to the joke, insisting instead:

"If you need something, tell me, please. At least some bread and ham for the trip. Ornella…"

Ornella rose, ready. The young man stood as well, lifting up his sack. He stood in silence for a moment and said:

"Thank you, but I don't need anything. If you'll allow me, though, I'll just give you a kiss."

And when the teacher poked his head out from the sheets, the young man bent over and kissed him on the forehead, damp with sweat. Then Ornella opened the door and he left.

Early the next morning, Ornella went to see the farmers to ask them to go summon the doctor. During the night, the teacher's fever had risen, and now he was gasping for breath.

"Who came to see you last night? The dog was agitated, even though he didn't bark."

"No one came," she stated brusquely.

The doctor didn't arrive until nearly noon, on a bicycle, with his coat of waterproof fabric all gleaming and dripping with rain.

His black, hooded figure seemed a bad omen to the sick man, but he wasn't upset by this deadly foreboding. He was tired. Perhaps God wanted to take him home and in so doing resolve the problems of his humble life. He surrendered to his illness with the sadness that illness brings to the flesh, but with a ray of hope in his soul, prepared for the great journey.

The doctor, however, encouraged him. He was practically an old man himself, tired and demure, who didn't trust his knowledge and went straight to the heart of his patient. In fact, the first thing he would do was listen to the heart, and if he found it physically strong, he would declare even a dying man to be out of danger.

"It's all a question of the heart," he told the teacher, covering him back up after a thorough examination. "A man suffers more or less, and causes more or less suffering, according to the constitution of his heart. It's pointless searching for the origin of our ailments, physical or moral, in other organs. When the heart is in good condition at the center of the body, giving precise orders to the blood, everything goes well. It's like the commander of an army. Your heart is good, so don't worry if a touch of bronchitis is giving you this shortness of breath. Try to sweat it out. Hot milk and wool blankets, that's all you need."

In the afternoon, the fever and shortness of breath worsened. Approaching the bed, Ornella felt like she was in front of the stove with the pot rumbling on top. The patient wasn't talking, nary a complaint even when his wheezing cough forced him to sit up, racked with pain. Frightened, she kept an eye on him, uncertain whether to send someone to notify his relatives or not.

This state of affairs made them both forget the prior evening's strange visit. Actually, in peaceful moments, when his thoughts took refuge from the oppression of his illness, the teacher confused the figure of the father-killer with the other people that the fever-induced nightmare sent wandering through his head. It had all been a dream. It was all a dream, and even his very life that was fading away like that sad, rainy day was nothing more than a dream.

57.

Given the situation, the farmers were more obliging and attentive than ever. Every so often they would come by to ask for news, and Gesuino lit a small lamp in front of a sacred image that he kept nailed next to his bed. Proto remembered that his wife used to cure all maladies with a brewed tea of dried lime flowers. He used it himself and thought it would be a good idea to prepare it for the teacher. He brought it steaming hot in a glass and had him drink it. Then he offered to stay the night to keep watch over him.

"No, no," the sick man said. "Tomorrow I'll be better."

The next day he was worse.

58.

Thus the days passed and he felt himself sliding down, down, as if the mattress macerated by his illness were sinking and becoming a hole. Outside the weather was sick as well. From the always black sky, rain fell continuously, accompanied by the rumble of the sea and the wind. Even Ornella had become pale and her damp hair looked dark. Fortunately, the farmers helped with everything. Under the cover of the big blue family umbrella, Proto went into town to buy groceries and when he returned, his shoes seemed like two boats just emerged from a stormy sea.

One evening he brough a small bottle, carefully wrapped in strongly scented white pharmacy paper, and naively said that he'd gone to consult the town's other doctor.

"'My brother Gesuino has bronchitis, can you prescribe something for me to give him?' I said, and he ordered this medicine. It's good for expectoration. One spoonful every hour. Here."

He took the bottle and set it on the chest of drawers. Then he asked Ornella for a spoon.

"Well done," the teacher said. "And you say you don't have faith in doctors and medicines."

"The one who came here kills people because he doesn't want to prescribe medicines," replied Proto to not contradict himself.

And he made the patient take a spoonful of the medicine, which was actually nothing more than innocent cough syrup for children.

That evening his recovery began.

59.

At that point the teacher allowed them to notify his family of his condition. Also, since the weather had cleared up, perhaps Marga would come pay him a visit.

Gesuino went, and returned somewhat embarrassed by the reply.

"Your daughter-in-law is coming right over, and she's bringing the girl as well. But…"

"But?"

Gesuino's mouth composed a sneer, directed at Ornella. "Well, it *would* be best if the girl didn't see Ornella in her condition."

"Why not?" the teacher asked. "Ola is too innocent to comprehend Ornella's condition. It's adults who ascribe their own malice to little children, awakening it in them."

But Ornella herself understood already and didn't want to be seen, especially by Marga. She also thought of getting back at Gesuino.

"If you don't mind, Gesuino, while you're here for a moment, I'll go wash some things at your well since there's still a bit of sun there."

And she went, without waiting for his permission. He watched her go with a nasty expression, annoyed by the thought that she was going to confer with Proto.

"What did Marga tell you?" the teacher asked, his voice turning frail and tremulous. But not even that modest voice could disarm Gesuino's disdain. With his yellowish leather overcoat and a cap, leather as well, lowered like a bonnet around his red face, entirely vexed as it was, he looked something like a primitive Eskimo.

Upset, he paced back and forth across the room, then stood in a wide stance in front of the bed.

"What did your daughter-in-law tell me? Nothing, that's what she told me. It seems she's been living under a rock. She seems to be totally in the dark about that girl's condition."

Since the teacher was looking at him, meek and silent, he exploded:

"And do you see how brazen that girl is? Why did she go do something at the well now? There's no sun left. She just wants to talk to Proto."

"So, let them talk. What's the harm in it?"

"No harm. People whisper, though. All in all, it would best if that girl stayed secluded in the house."

"But just now it was you who implied she should leave."

"She could have retreated up to the loft," said Gesuino, looking up tragically. The teacher smiled, but briefly, because the other man asked with brutal candor: "Where will you have her give birth?"

"Jesus was born in a stable. God will provide."

Gesuino went purple in the face, all the way down to his neck. He grumbled: "God... God..." Then he seemed to change the subject. "Your daughter-in-law told me that her husband has been away since last week, on business, and that's why he hasn't shown up."

"It doesn't matter. And tell me, Gesuino, was it she who suggested that you send Ornella away?"

"Didn't I tell you that she doesn't know, or pretends not to know a thing?" Impatiently he added: "Although everyone knows." Once again struck by the notion of a possible conversation between Proto and Ornella, he went to look out the door.

"Let the rumors fly," the teacher insisted. "They'll be getting married one of these days anyway. What do you say? Do you consent?"

"God's will be done," said the farmer, turning around in resignation.

Then the teacher expressed the thought Gesuino had just hinted at.

"God, God, yes, fine, but we're burdening God with all the responsibilities that might inconvenience us."

"Yes, it's true. You're exactly right."

"Well then, one of you must marry Ornella. Will it be Proto? Will it be you?"

"I've never liked venison," said Gesuino with a disgusted grimace. He seemed to regret having already said too much and decided not to continue. But after sitting next to the fire and bending over to stoke it, he felt an overpowering urge to state one of his intentions: "If my brother does make that stupid mistake, I can guarantee you one thing: that girl will walk the straight and narrow. I'll see to that, blast it all to hell!"

The arrival of Marga and Ola prevented the teacher from offering his observations. Besides, all the world's ills were forgotten when Ola's presence lit up the air around her. And in fact, her little red wool dress radiated a sense of light and warmth.

When the grandfather took her tiny hands in his, though, they were cold, as if they'd been buried in ice. Even the tip of her little nose, brushing against his face, felt like a chilled fruit. But from her red mouth came a warm mist like one that rises from the earth at dawn in the spring, and her eyes were reminiscent of the rising sun.

"I won't kiss you to prevent infecting you with this malady," said the grandfather, pushing her away in spite of himself. "Go sit by the fire and warm yourself up."

Ola, however, was looking with diffidence at the big, hairy, yellowish figure of Gesuino, still bent over, blowing on the fire.

"No, he's not an ogre. Go on, Ola."

"Who is he then?" she said with her frank impudence. And that's all it took for the grandfather, after so much time, to laugh. The wrinkles that pain and illness had etched onto his face were shining now like ruts after the rain when the sun returns.

Marga looked from one to the other without curiosity, serene and cold. Her winter dress, in black velvet trimmed with an awkward gold lace, gave her the air of a lady from long ago. Even her smooth face, unusually flushed from the cold, and from around which her white wool scarf had come loose, looked lacquered and painted.

"Why didn't you send for me right away?" she scolded sweetly. "Antonio has been off since last week because he's trying to arrange to ship fish directly to regional wholesalers. I've been a bit under the weather myself, and no one told me about you."

"It doesn't matter," he said, rising up a bit to see Ola better. "The boat has righted itself and everything is improving. What did you bring in that package? Remember, Marga, that I don't need anything."

"It was Ola. It was you, right, Ola, who wanted to bring something for your grandfather? Turn around this way a little and stand still! What am I going to do with you?"

Ola wanted to climb up to the loft, and when they didn't let her, she asked where Ornella was. Told that she was at the farmers' washing clothes, Ola asked if she could go to her. That's when Gesuino stood up, offering to accompany her.

"Oh, Gesuino!" exclaimed the teacher, with a menacing wave of his hand. "You must know, Marga, that our Gesuino is in love with Ornella."

Marga didn't laugh, didn't speak, but from the way she turned to look at the farmer, as if seeing him for the first time, and under extraordinary circumstances, the teacher realized that his joke had aroused a profound hope in her.

Gesuino didn't deny it. He stood there firmly planted in front of the fireplace, determined to never betray his inner yearnings again.

60.

That same evening the letter carrier who was rarely seen in those parts brought a registered letter for Ornella to the farmers who directed him to the teacher. She took the letter herself, looking at it carefully front and back. With an almost rapacious movement, she tore into the envelope and opened the sheet of paper to see the signature and then quickly read what was written on it. Then she read it again, slowly, too slowly, as if she were unable to decipher the words, stopping every so often like someone studying the path they were about to walk down. Finally she said:

"It's that idiot cousin of mine who's a soldier, and he's writing to me because he says that he hasn't gotten a letter from home in two months."

She left the letter on the table, as if it were unimportant to her, and the teacher didn't ask to read it and didn't comment. He didn't, however, believe a single word she'd said. Who was writing her? Maybe Antonio, under a different name.

She didn't say anything more either, but her every movement revealed hidden agitation. The first thing she did was look at herself in the little mirror the teacher used when he shaved, smoothing her hair down with both hands. Then she began wandering around the room aimlessly, moving objects she never touched and then putting them back again, stopping every so often in front of the window, bewildered like a fly that deludes itself into thinking it can go through the glass. Finally, she climbed up into the loft only to come right back down, and the first thing she laid eyes on was the letter.

"Tomorrow I need to go to his house and let them know," she said, refolding the letter and putting it in her deep pocket. She knitted her brow, feigning annoyance.

Later, when she went to close the gate, she returned with a sardonic smile, eyes gleaming with malice.

"Those two numbskulls are fighting, and how! I've never seen them so angry. Gesuino is like a bull."

"Why are they fighting?"

"I don't know. Do you hear them? Their voices are carrying all the way here. They're going to kill each other tonight."

Knowing she was the cause, she laughed, slightly bent over, as if needing to suppress her depraved hilarity.

From the bed where shadows, gold-tinged by the fire, were already extending their veil, the teacher watched her and guessed everything. The two brothers were fighting over who would eventually have her, and she was laughing because she'd never belong to either of them. The letter tucked in her pocket, the one she kept touching, must have guaranteed a different, better future for her. But who was offering it? The mystery nettled the teacher. But he decided to hold his tongue and lie low in order to find out.

She stayed up until a late hour, seemingly calm now, sitting next to the table, knitting. She was making some wool socks for him, and it had been her idea. Every now and then, she demonstrated true thoughtfulness, and she had been knitting these socks with a certain passion, measuring one against the other so that they'd turn out equal and precise. That night, however, she was proceeding mechanically, with no thought but to finish them.

"Ornella," he said suddenly, thinking out loud. "You should be concentrating on making a layette set for the baby instead."

"I was thinking about it," she replied without looking up. "Tomorrow when I deliver my cousin's letter, I'll buy some fabric in the piazza."

He mulled that over. She was planning to go out, but where? She'd never mentioned this cousin of hers or any other relative before.

When she was up in the loft, she didn't put out the light like she usually did. Then the teacher, who she thought had dozed off, relit his and noticed that the inkwell and paper were missing.

The next morning, when Proto came to enquire after them, he sent Ornella to buy groceries and asked the farmer to stay with him a moment. The man was happy to. His brow was furrowed and his eyes swollen, like he'd spent a rough night, and he wanted to let off some steam.

"Did you hear that bedlam last night? I'm starting to think that my brother Gesuino is possessed by the devil. I'm serious. I'm not superstitious, but I recall tales my mother used to tell. She said that souls of the damned wander the world, slipping into the bodies of simple people. And I think Gesuino was possessed by the soul of the father killed by his sons here."

"I see. But then how do you react to him? Are you possessed as well?"

"That's true," said Proto. "You're absolutely right."

"That's one good quality you both share: you always say I'm right, but then you keep hurting each other. What were you fighting about last night?"

"Who knows? Gesuino came back from here in a ferocious mood. He started by beating the dog, and, naturally, I protested. That led to the quarrel."

"Listen, Proto," the teacher said after a moment of silence, "I still need you. Yesterday evening Ornella received a registered letter, and last night she replied. I need to know who sent the letter."

"I saw it. It came from Genoa, and the handwriting belongs to an educated person. Why didn't you ask her yourself?"

"I don't want to smother her. It only makes things worse."

"Forget about her. Let her go back to the hell where she came from."

"There's a baby involved—we need to save the baby."

"To hell with the baby as well!" Proto exploded, pounding his fist on the table. "You're too old-fashioned. You'll see where she ends up one day, you'll see."

Nothing intimidated the teacher, not even the string of curses and vituperation that the farmer was muttering against Ornella, Gesuino, God, and mankind in general. Instead, he was entertaining a new thought: If the letter came from Genoa, and the handwriting was that of an educated person, could it have been from Adelmo Bianchi? Anything was possible when it came to that head full of wind.

He reconstructed the scene of that first evening of his illness. Once again he saw the father-killer looking at Ornella with his crazed eyes, and he no longer had a doubt.

216

"Proto," he whispered, "we must keep an eye on the girl. I want to know where she's going and what she's doing this morning."

The farmer was overcome by his own curiosity, and resentment drove him to spy on Ornella in order to possibly get back at her.

"Have no doubt—come noon, I'll be able to tell you everything. And now I'm off."

By noon the teacher already knew that Ornella had indeed been to the house of some relatives, and then had bought some fabric from a merchant in the piazza, and finally, had gone into the post office.

61.

That same day, bad weather resumed. Like an army that after a brief respite hurls itself against the enemy with renewed vigor, the rain, wind, cold, and even snow raged all around the cursed house.

Despite it all, the teacher got up. The socks Ornella had knitted, a shawl Marga had given him on behalf of Ola, and an old wool cap of his were of great benefit in completing his winter accoutrement. Thus camouflaged, he looked at himself in the mirror and felt like winter personified. And yet, inside, he felt completely renewed, with resolute intentions for the future.

He sat next to the fire and read back issues of the newspaper, but he never took his eye off Ornella, waiting for the opportune moment to try to save her from the new peril towards which she was blindly heading.

62

Ornella never approached the fire once. When she finished her chores, she sat next to the table and was sewing the layette for her little one. He heard her heavy breathing and still wasn't convinced that she was silently plotting something sinister.

At times he wondered if it wasn't better, as Proto advised, to leave her to her own devices and her own instincts which, after all, in a self-centered animal such as she, could only be to her benefit. After all, no blood ties bound them, and if he was only keeping her there out of fear that she would resume her former tragedy, and also to atone for it, and if she now had a way to save herself and live better somewhere else, then there was no reason to stop her.

But no, that wasn't it. Deep down he felt there *was* another reason, that there was a bond, stronger than that of blood. He wanted to keep her baby because it was linked to the baby he'd fathered and killed, and so was the continuation of his own life. And he wanted it in order to instill true life in it, a life of goodness, while if Ornella took it away, she would teach it only evil.

That point established, he was determined to fight in order to give himself a reason to live and the strength to preserve the light of goodness within.

And so he resumed his attempts to morally seduce Ornella by describing to her the simple, picturesque life of that far-away village. It was an ancient, modest, crumbling portrait that he restored with the colors and varnish of his imagination.

"This time of year we have cold and snow too, but it's different. The cold is dry, and the snow hardens and sparkles like alabaster. Everything is pure and alive. And inside my little house, which I hope to recover shortly, one lives magnificently. There's the kitchen with a hearth that ten people can nestle under. The dining room overlooks the valley, while the upstairs rooms have windows facing the mountain. On clear days you can see the courageous hunters climbing the trails through the rocks. They're dressed in leather and look like rulers of the forest. They belong to the richest families of the land, and they compete in swiftness and daring. There's one, my pupil, who doesn't even touch the beast he shoots. He has a beater, one of his servants, take it away, and if the meat is good, like deer or boar for example, he sends it as a gift to his friends, like the king does. Often, at night, he would come see me, and then there were incredible tales of beasts he'd heard tell of, birds stealing gems and gold coins and hiding them, wolves that used to be men. Once…"

He attempted to repeat the extraordinary tales of the young hunter, getting drawn up in the sound of his own words and weaving his scant memories of real life into details of hunting events he'd read in adventure novels. It was the only way to attack the woman's savage soul, and he would carefully pause right at the climax, leaving her shocked and in suspense, to then resume with greater assurance. That was how the tortoise did it when it attacked, biting carefully, a poisonous spider.

Sometimes the farmers came in the evening, and Gesuino would bring freshly roasted chestnuts in a scalding hot handkerchief.

"Smell that," he would say, holding it next to Ornella's neck, but she should lean away, avoiding it with disdain. Ever since she'd received the registered letter, she stopped letting the farmers joke around with her. Without a word, she put the chestnuts on a plate, poured the wine like the teacher asked, and then returned to her spot next to the table where she sewed and sewed, stopping only to thread the needle in the light or to untangle, using her teeth, knots that the irritating thread formed on its own.

When those two were there, the teacher didn't resume his stories. He felt it was wasted effort because she wasn't paying attention, under the sway of her inner voice of opposition instead. Her very treatment of the farmers, detached and disdainful of contact, revealed her isolation. They in turn seemed intent only on their own conversation, but he noticed that from time to time Gesuino would look at Ornella from the corner of his eye, as if ready to throw a lasso around her if she tried to run off.

"He'll end up marrying her," the teacher thought, and the idea that the story would turn out that way amused him, but deep down in his soul he remained sad because, sadly, whatever happened, it was still the same old story.

Part IV

♦◇♦

The Birth

63.

Now one of those evenings, as Gesuino was bending over to toss blackened chestnut shells onto the fire and Proto was drinking his second glass of wine in slow, blissful sips, he heard a knocking at the door.

Ornella was trembling all over, like she'd suddenly awakened in a fright, but didn't get up. Gesuino stood and went to the door with a scowl, as if a wolf were out there, and opened without asking who it was.

As if pushed by a gust of wind, a tall, hooded figure entered, black raincoat glistening wet. At first the teacher thought it was the doctor, but quickly realized it was Antonio.

"You weren't expecting my visit," he said, with a mixture of mirth and tragedy, but still in a measured tone. "And I beg your pardon, sir farmers, for having passed through your gate, but it was plainly open."

"True, very true," admitted Proto. "But then our gate is always open."

Gesuino opened his mouth to speak, but nothing came out. Recovered from his initial surprise, he watched Antonio from behind as he casually removed his overcoat. Then he looked at Ornella who had turned red down to her fingernails. He finally sat back down.

A moment of silence followed.

Outside, the wind pierced and tore the web of rain, slamming it against the walls of the house with a metallic sound, and the teacher felt that the moisture was seeping into the room.

Antonio looked for somewhere to put his coat. Finding nothing else, he tossed it on the stairs to the loft, and in the shadows, the garment looked like a fallen spirit.

Proto meanwhile had finished drinking his wine. He stood to set the glass on the table and took a quick look at Ornella as well. She seemed so distant and lost in thought that he said to himself:

"Hey, old friend, you and your brother Gesuino are intruding here. Time to go."

He made his way to the fireplace and pressed his finger into his brother's back.

"Let's go, Gesuino. It's late."

Since no one was keeping them, after saying goodbye to everyone with a certain embarrassment, the two brothers left.

Just like during the father-killer's visit, the teacher felt he was dreaming. And yet, it seemed Antonio brought a whiff of cruel reality, forcing those dreams to collapse like that black fabric ghost on the stairs to the loft.

"Marga and Ola say hello," Antonio said, taking Gesuino's chair. He stretched his legs out, with their long, snug leather boots.

Those names and that greeting softened the teacher's heart. His face brightened. His spirits lifted. He was back in control of events.

Then he noticed that Antonio had changed physically, like someone who'd suffered an illness or spent a long time in a foreign country. His face had hardened, and while maintaining its classic features, it had taken on a different expression, like that of a statue retouched by a dissatisfied sculptor. His hair, earlier styled with a feminine part, now was straight, compact, shaved on his powerful neck. And his eyes, although fixed on the fire, no longer sparkled, motionless under brows that knitted and smoothed as if following the up-and-down movement of the flames.

Once the farmers had gone, even his voice shed its habitual mask of theatrical enunciation as he conveyed Marga and Ola's greetings. And after getting good and settled in front of the fire with his arms crossed, he brusquely stated:

"I came to resolve this matter of Ornella." Each word seemed to drop straight to floor and burst open like certain hard fruit when the rind is ripe.

Neither of the two replied. In fact, Ornella hunched down even further, no longer feeling like a person, but like an object in his hands.

He continued: "We've become the laughing-stock of the town. All of them, starting with my wife, know the truth and pretend they don't, not out of respect, but out of fear of me, of my fists, obviously. But they're all laughing about it. They're laughing because they're jealous, that's obvious too. If I were a poor wretch or my wife a shrew, they wouldn't pay any attention to me or my business. Fortunately, that's not how things stand. That is to say, I am what I am, and my wife is a prudent woman. But I know she's suffering as well, and that she also deserves respect, not false compassion and concealed ridicule from her fellow man, and I want this scandal to end."

"You just now became aware of all this?" the teacher asked.

"Yes, sir! If I'd realized it sooner, I would've remedied it sooner."

"It's better avoided than remedied."

"We're not born with our teeth. In fact, as they say, wisdom comes with the loss of our teeth, our adult ones, of course."

"Well then, let's hear what you intend to do."

"Something very simple: take Ornella to a home for unwed mothers, far from here, and where I've already reserved a spot, and await the baby's birth."

"And then?"

"And then provide for them: *If you break it, you pay for it.*"

"So you'd have two families."

"If need be, I'll have two families and work for them both. I wouldn't be the first, nor the last."

"Does your wife know of your decision?"

"She'll find out, probably, since she devilishly guesses even my most secret intentions, but as usual she'll hold her tongue and let me do as I please, thoroughly convinced that I'm not an awful scoundrel like people think. She only talked to me about you, begging me to do whatever it takes so you can come home to us. I gave her my word, and I expect to keep that promise."

The teacher didn't immediately respond. He seemed to be again searching for the best solution to the affair and again finding only one possibility.

"I'll return to my hometown, where I'm already in negotiations to get my house back. Ornella will come with me, and if necessary, I'll give her and the baby my name."

Antonio began to laugh, but quickly squeezed and wrung his hands a bit as if to suppress his *schadenfreude*, and then became sad again.

"That's a lot of romantic hogwash that no one around here subscribes to."

"Where I'm from they still do," the teacher insisted, gathering strength.

"No, not even there anymore. These days people are practical and laugh at the poor souls who waste their time beating a dead horse."

"Forget that, let them laugh. Explain to me how this is like beating a dead horse."

"Because two months wouldn't go by before Ornella would either run away from your home or cheat on you with your best friend."

This time she was the one to stifle a snicker. The two men's debate perked her up. She raised her head and resumed sewing, thinking of a way to help the teacher free her from Antonio's tyranny. When the time was right, she would take care of things herself, but her plans were so mysterious and hidden that when she saw her lover ferreting them out, she felt like a guilty prisoner all over again.

The teacher was saying: "Let's set the future aside and discuss the present. Actually, let's discuss your change of heart. How is it that you've gone from kicking Ornella out to wanting her as practically a second wife?"

He leaned forward considerably, speaking with a soft, deep voice, as if not wanting Ornella to hear.

"And you've never changed your mind? You've never regretted anything bad you've done? I too have suffered over these past months. And you would be disavowing the principles that you taught me as a boy if you truly believed me to be an insensitive villain. I turned thirty yesterday," he said, abruptly standing. "It's time to mend my ways. And to learn self-respect. Sometimes self-esteem and pride can turn even scoundrels into men of conscience. And while we're on the subject of scoundrels, I have to tell you that there's an ugly creep involved in this story as well. One night you received a visit from Adelmo Bianchi, the parricide."

The teacher reflexively turned and looked at Ornella. He caught a glimpse of her, head hunched down again, almost touching the fabric, in the posture she assumed when she wanted to hide her thoughts. And he understood everything.

Without turning back toward the fire, he answered with a different voice, strong and resolute.

"Yes, Bianchi was here one night, before my illness. Why?"

"First, why don't you tell me what he came for."

"How would I know? To say goodbye to his house, he said, before leaving the country."

"Let me tell you! That man is so brazen, he never opens his mouth unless he's telling a lie. On top of that, he's evil, just look at what he's done. Well, after visiting you, he really did leave that night—he went to Genoa without a coin in his pocket because he always manages to wriggle out of any tight spot and slip away like a fox. In Genoa he found work at the port and learned to be a cook because he's planning to take a job as such in a merchant steamer bound for South America. He got a false passport, but before embarking, he's waiting for Miss Ornella to pack her things and meet him there."

Like at the beginning of the conversation, neither of the other two spoke. The teacher kept watching Ornella. He saw her lift her head with a certain dignity, quickly bowing it again under his gaze.

Unruffled, Antonio continued:

"He wrote her a registered letter that you may have seen. He in fact suggested that she meet him as soon as possible, procuring a passport first, naturally. And who knows what all he led her to believe. She replied, agreeing, and was waiting for her papers to be ready before leaving with her things packed."

Her with her things packed! Those words hurt the teacher like punches. An ignoble, humiliating pain. And he didn't know what deep-seated urge for revenge made him want to hurt Antonio back.

"Now I understand the motive for your actions. Hardly self-respect—it's jealousy."

And maybe it was, because Antonio was dispassionate. He simply remarked:

"Oh, it's not self-respect? What if one day the father-killer gets caught, and probably his companion along with him, and in the trial that's currently postponed because they're still searching for Bianchi and hope to catch him, our name and this whole ridiculous story of ours are mentioned, do you think that would be a fine thing?"

"Excuse me," said the teacher, "but how did you find out about this?"

"That's not important. The facts are known."

"But are you sure this is true?"

Then Antonio spun about, as if sitting on a swivel chair, and pointed at Ornella in a contemptuous gesture.

"Ask *her* if it's true or not."

That seemed to mark the start of Ornella's trial.

"Ornella," said the teacher, "you did, it's true, receive a registered letter, but you said it was from a cousin. How do you respond now to Antonio's assertions?"

"The letter I received really was from my cousin," she replied, continuing to sew as she feigned a certain indifference. "You can go ask my relatives."

"Cousin? What cousin!" Antonio shouted, losing his patience. "You might be able to bamboozle this paragon of virtue here, but not me. You have no cousins, and of course those 'relatives' of yours are backing you up in this ugly affair. And that no-account lowlife of your aunt is the one in charge of getting your papers made."

"Those papers," she said calmly, "are needed so I can go away with the teacher."

Antonio cursed with a mixture of scorn and amusement and said:

"I knew you were brazen, but not to this degree. And tell me something. Last Saturday morning you were at the post office and collected a second letter to which you sent an express, registered response on Monday. Was that correspondence with your 'cousin' as well?"

Ornella didn't respond. The teacher intervened again.

"Ornella, we don't want to hurt you. In fact, you see we're here competing for you like Helen of Troy. You should tell the truth out of gratitude at least. Besides, if you're planning on leaving, no one is going to—"

"No, not that," Antonio interrupted, already fed up. "I stated my intention and I'm not changing my mind. I just need to say and repeat one more thing: if after the birth of the baby, you want to hang yourself, or worse, run away with that imbecile, that's your choice. But my son, I'm taking charge of him."

"Think it over, Ornella."

"Where did you put Bianchi's letters?"

"Oh, you're so annoying!" she exclaimed with sudden courage. She let the diaper she was hemming drop to the floor and pulled two letters, folded together, from her deep pocket. She acted like she was going to drop those as well, but then set them on the table.

"Give me those letters," ordered Antonio with his dictatorial master's voice, and when he got his hands on them, he examined the envelopes. The first was addressed to the Bianchi house, the second had been sent via general delivery. So he had been correctly informed after all.

"Read them aloud." It was the teacher giving the order this time.

In the gloomy room where that seemingly drab, vulgar drama was playing out, a breath of the poetry and airy spaces that only the imagination can reach lingered still, thanks to the criminal, the father-killer, the "lowest of the low."

My dearest Ornella, forgive me for taking the liberty of addressing you so informally, as though we were intimate, but ever since the night I saw my sad, cursed house again, I haven't stopping talking to you, and you're following me on my eventful journey. We talk all day, and at night we sleep together wrapped in the same cloud of dreams.

Ornella, my fate is perhaps like that of the 'Wandering Jew,' who must always restart his journey around the world, when his world is nothing more than a little garden, which in the long run feels like a prison. His only remaining solace from despair is to gaze at the stars or ask the sun to melt him with its light. But even that is denied him, and he must live for eternity, to suffer in eternity. He wanted to challenge the love of God, standing in opposition to the laws that govern human life, and so his punishment is to be banished from those human laws. He's not allowed to die, but he's no longer allowed to live. That's how I am…

At that point, Antonio, who in spite of himself had gotten caught up in the sound of his own voice, asked with a touch of both irony and curiosity:

"What in the devil did this man do?"

"When Christ on the road to Calvary stumbled under the weight of the cross, one of the bystanders said: 'Hey! Get up and walk!' And then Jesus, rising up, said: 'And you'll walk for eternity,'" the teacher explained solemnly. "That's Ahasuerus, the Wandering Jew."

Antonio continued reading:

That's how I am if you, Ornella, deny me your presence. If you come with me, mother-wife-sister, then I'll be reborn. I'll be like the innocent creature that's bound to be born from you, and both of us—I and your baby, who'll be mine as well—will live in you and in your love.

I swear to you, Ornella, that I won't plant so much as a kiss on your fingertips until you've fulfilled your sacred duty as a mother, and I'll surround you with my care and attention. I'll lie at your feet like a faithful dog and you'll be able to sleep in peace even if a storm is thundering around us or if our house is surrounded by lions.

"Criminy!" shouted Antonio, but he wasn't laughing and his eyes never left the letter.

It was divine inspiration that led me back to my sad house that night. I had the idea that the fire was still burning there and that the placated spirits of my parents were waiting to forgive and bless me. And I wanted to take some memento away with me: the ocarina that had accompanied my earliest dreams of love with its plaintive melody, my mother's wedding ring. And the fire, I did find it, in your golden eyes, Ornella, and the music and the wedding ring, I took those away in my young boy's heart, along with my love for you, Ornella. Ornella! When I pronounce that name, I still hear the rustling of the alders near the sun-drenched vineyard, in the middle of the summer days when the grapes begin to turn red and the nightingale pecks at the ripe fig to make his song even sweeter. We'll go far, Ornella, but if you'll love me, everywhere, even to the deserts or the muddy cities, and we'll rediscover the summer vineyard, and the nightingale will sing in our hearts.

64.

The teacher listened attentively, taut like a string ready to vibrate, in fact. In place of Antonio, ruddy and bursting with both genuine and mock laughter, the teacher pictured the sad, scrawny father-killer and thought about the effect that his words must have had on the woman, coming as they did from the other man's mouth. From the corner of his eye, he saw her, though, bent over her sewing, with only a faint crease of disgust surrounding her disdainful mouth. Noticing she was being watched, she seemed to erase even that superficial expression and close herself up in a shell of complete indifference.

The second letter spoke of practical things, confirming the news that Antonio had related. The parricide was working at the port in Genoa, and was in negotiations to get in as a cook onboard a large transatlantic liner. He was waiting for Ornella, who, despite finding herself in the condition she was in, had apparently promised to meet him as soon as possible.

65.

"Wonderful!" exclaimed Antonio, refolding the two letters together and stuffing them in his pants pocket. Then he stood a moment, deep in thought, frowning. It had grown quiet outside as well, and in the room's sudden silence, it felt like the gray night was looking in through the window to take part in the tragedy.

Indeed, the story took on the color of tragedy when Antonio, his entire body shaking like a warrior who'd inadvertently nodded off when he was supposed to leave for battle, said curtly:

"And now, Ornella, get your things and let's go. Early tomorrow morning," he added, addressing the teacher, "Marga will send the servant here, for anything you need."

Ornella didn't look up, but stopped sewing, with the needle still stuck into the fabric. Her bearing reminded the teacher of a tortoise that thinks it's being chased and stops, prepared to retreat entirely into its shell.

He too was silent. He felt that they'd arrived at a crossroads in the murky night, and only intuition could save them. He waited for Ornella to speak, as she was the most intuitive of the three. She pulled the needle from the fabric and then jabbed it back in with rage. Then she boldly lifted her head.

"I'm not going."

But Antonio didn't lose his temper. He turned back to the teacher.

"You convince her. I know you'll do your duty."

"No one knows my duty better than I do. Ornella must remain here, and I'll persuade her to do her duty as well."

"You're deluded, and you'll always be deluded. Forgive me for speaking so frankly. Three days won't pass before Ornella runs away. And for crying out loud, I won't allow my son to be born on the street and travel the world with lowlifes and gypsies."

"If she's going to run away, then she'll run away just the same from the house where you're taking her."

"Absolutely not! I know who I'm dealing with. Besides, I'll say it again: once the baby is born, she'll be free to do as she pleases. Have I made myself clear?" he yelled at her. "So get moving!"

She didn't move. Now her eyes were fixed on the teacher as if her destiny depended on him and not the other man. But even he found himself back in a circle of fog, and in Antonio's tone he had heard such unshakeable determination that he didn't know what to do. He instinctively turned back towards Ornella, and responding to what her expression was begging of him, he calmly said:

"Ornella, you must be free to make your own decision. I can no longer come between you and Antonio. You two share responsibility for your baby, and everything must be done for its safety and salvation."

"I want to stay here, at least a few days. I don't want to be forced," she said, but Antonio didn't let her continue.

"Well, I am going to force you to come with me, right now. I know you too well, and everything has to be settled immediately."

"What if I don't want to go? What if I scream?"

"Don't test my patience, Ornella. You remember the taste of my fists."

As he said that, Antonio approached her, as if to better display his tall stature and remind her of his strength, or perhaps even to reawaken her carnal desire for his body, the one thing that could convince her to follow him.

Ornella didn't budge; her expression didn't change. Cold and hard, she held the needle, her sole weapon.

Then he really did lose his patience. He grabbed her shoulder like a rock he wanted to hurl far away and gave it a good shake. The fabric slipped from her lap, and in the tragic silence they heard the clink of one of her hairpins falling on the floor.

The teacher stood, leaning with his hand on the chair like he did when he would prepare to call his undisciplined pupils at school to order, but the intended composure and sternness abandoned him from all sides, replaced by a nervous tremor that began shaking him when he saw Ornella resisting Antonio's force, and then the man punched her between the shoulders.

Finally the teacher approached and grabbed the man's arm. Antonio abruptly turned, surprised, as if he'd completely forgotten about him. He flushed with rage.

"Get out of the way," he said, pushing the man, and not gently. "You've stuck your nose in our business enough." Turning to Ornella, he repeated: "Get up! Get up or I'll no longer be responsible for my actions."

When she didn't obey, he pulled something from his pocket, squeezing it in his fist like a key: a little revolver.

66.

Ornella immediately stood, and with the listless gait of a wild beast intimidated by its tamer, she headed to the stairs.

The teacher returned to his chair beside the fireplace, facing the flames. He didn't want to look at Antonio again. He felt that everything really was finished now. The matter weighing on his conscience had disappeared the way embers disappear in the fireplace: into fire and ash. He almost laughed at himself, thinking of all that long, pointless suffering, but it was a bitter laughter that wanted to escape, because deep down, sorrow was weighing on him more than ever.

Meanwhile, he heard Ornella up in the loft, moving about, changing her dress and gathering her things. Antonio put his hat on as well and approached the fireplace. With a troubled voice he said:

"You will forgive me if I was rough. But it was necessary. I must tell you," he added softly, leaning over the teacher, "that Marga was the one who compelled me to do this, to get her out of a ridiculous, upsetting situation."

"You don't have to bother with me anymore, not you, not Marga, not anyone else," replied the teacher, unwaveringly staring at the fire. "I don't know anyone anymore."

"You'll calm down and see that things will work out. After all, I'm doing my duty and following the path you yourself once laid out for me. Don't you remember? You wanted me to get Ornella out of my house and out of the town where my family lives and to find a solution for the baby that was arriving. Isn't that what you wanted? And that's what I'm doing."

Since the teacher didn't seem convinced, much less satisfied, Antonio straightened up impatiently and continued:

"Don't you understand that I'm more your son than you can possibly imagine? I know everything: about you, your past, the bond that unites us. Marga told me, and now there's three of us, fighting against evil so that Ola will be spared any residual punishment."

The teacher looked up, and just as the fire's glow cast a bloody reflection on Antonio's bright clothing, he had yet another hallucination: he saw the dead woman again, the baby inside her.

"Ola is safe now," he said. "The one who will certainly be lost is Ornella's child."

Then he didn't speak again, not even when Ornella came down with her bundle of things, setting it on the table to finish packing. First she tossed in her slippers, and then the cloth diaper that was still on the floor, after shaking and refolding it. At last she looked around, calm and indifferent, eyes searching for something she may have forgotten. She gazed for a moment at the little scene of *The Flight into Egypt*, but quickly looked down. In her own plans to fly off and join the father-killer, she'd thought about taking the picture with her. She didn't even know why. Perhaps because it was the only thing of value in the house.

She worried the teacher would guess what she was thinking, and so to throw him off, she bent over to search for the lost hairpin. A moment later when she straightened back up, she looked different, with her face as yellow as her braids and her big eyes filled with fear. She raised her arms to pull her hair up and replace the pin, but it must have poked into her neck because she let out a bellow that sounded like an ox receiving a killing blow from a butcher's club.

The two men thought it was a pretense, but she collapsed onto the chair and pressed her forehead onto the bundle, clenching her teeth to keep from screaming again.

A moment later a second shriek seemed to fill the room with thunder and fright. It was a strange scream, one that arose from her bowels as if coming from a subterranean place where frightening things occurred, and it begged for help, and at the same time was a curse.

"Ornella," said Antonio, frightened. But she waved her arms, like a tormented bird's wings, to both drive him away and to hurt him in revenge.

"Go away, go away," she said in a hoarse voice. "Vile, despicable criminal, get away from me!"

A profound hatred resonated in that raspy voice, a broader lament than that of her earlier cries. It was the ancient hatred of a woman for the man who compelled her to procreate, who, for his own pleasure, pierced her flesh and turned her womb into a nest of pain.

The teacher understood and rose to his feet.

"It's the pain of childbirth," he said with simplicity. "We must go find the midwife. Get up, Ornella, and come lie down on my bed."

He took her by the arm and forced her to stand. She perked up and with his support took a few steps toward the bed, but then changed her mind, slipped from his grasp, and practically crawled up the little staircase to the loft, like an animal hiding away to give birth.

67

Despite his heroic intentions, Antonio didn't feel up to the task of going in search of the midwife. In fact, he thought that for the sake of his self-respect, it might be a good time to beat a hasty retreat.

And so, Proto was sent to summon the midwife. Proto made the best of everything, but this task in particular sounded enjoyable to him. He considered playing a trick on the midwife by leading her to believe it was a very mysterious case, a foreign woman who had come to give birth in the country to cover up her sin. He laughed to himself, under the dome of his big umbrella, pummeled by the rain, as he walked in the dark along the muddy street.

He returned rather humiliated, however. The midwife was attending to another childbirth, for rich people, and knowing quite well who Proto was representing, she had greeted him with cold hostility.

"She'll come when she's finished there."

"I see that it's up to me to act as midwife as well," the teacher said happily. He'd already opened Ornella's bundle of belongings and took out the baby smocks and diapers she'd made. And he went about recalling what he'd read in some scientific book about how one should attend to a woman in labor.

Proto looked on attentively. Seeing Ornella's few things— shirts, slippers, stockings—scattered on the table almost felt like an affront to his modesty. But they also provoked a sense of distress, as if they were the clothing left on the seashore by someone intending to drown herself.

"Still, we must help the poor girl," he said. "We need to give her something to drink."

"There's a quick remedy!" the teacher exclaimed, poking fun at the farmer's naiveté.

There was a sudden knock on the door. Both men raced to open it, hoping it was the midwife, and both men smiled at seeing Gesuino's bewildered face. Overcome by a painfully unbearable curiosity, he'd put his overcoat and cap back on and was coming to see. In the short distance between their place and the teacher's, he'd gotten soaked by the rain and was now shivering from the cold like a frostbitten dog.

"What do you want?" his brother asked tartly, trying to keep him from entering. "Go home."

But the teacher decided to put Gesuino's goodwill to the test as well, and handing him the family umbrella, he said:

"Proto went to summon that slatternly midwife, but she refused to come right away. We'll lodge a complaint, but meanwhile, Gesuino, go to the doctor on my behalf and beg him to come. Two lives hang in the balance."

Gesuino took the umbrella and abruptly opened it there on the doorstep, brandishing it like a shield against the rain's fury, and then he raced off.

"Poor fellow. My brother's a good man after all," Proto said, more to himself than to the teacher.

68.

It was a memorable night for everyone. Outside the rain was pouring down incessantly, as if trying to violently isolate the teacher's dwelling from the rest of the world in order to deprive the guilty woman of any assistance.

But the wilder the elements' oppression, the more tenacity the men demonstrated in overcoming their momentary difficulties.

Gesuino returned, accompanied by the physician who had once treated the teacher, and after examining Ornella, the good doctor said it was a case of premature labor, undoubtedly provoked by some exertion or something that had greatly upset the woman. The teacher didn't mention Antonio's visit.

Every so often he would climb up to the loft. Ornella was still dressed, sometimes lying down, sometimes sitting up on the low bed, which was in complete disarray. In the light of a tallow candle whose flame quivered and stretched as if dancing in the air, her figure appeared as a dark outline against the white wall background, and when she sat up, with her head lowered onto her crossed arms, she looked like a prisoner gnawing at her chains.

Indeed, the small room with its slit-like window, upside-down crate for table and chair, and chamber pot under the bed did resemble a prison cell.

The teacher couldn't recall ever having laid eyes on such a gloomy scene. The rain thundering on the roof sounded like a tempest of lapilli unleashed on the house by a volcanic eruption, and death was there, visible, in Ornella's own shadow. Nevertheless, he felt a mysterious sense of joy in the depths of his entire being. That night like never before, the presence and power of God were revealed to him. God with his staff was marking the boundary between man's will and his impotence when it came to forging his destiny. God was abolishing time, space, and death itself to make him believe that Ornella was the woman whose womb once held his seed, that the woman he had killed all those years ago was being returned to him.

69.

The doctor had gone, giving assurances that the delivery was bound to occur towards dawn, and that he would personally take it upon himself to compel the midwife to do her duty.

Hours passed. The two farmers took turns at the teacher's side. No one spoke, as if instead of watching over a woman in labor, they were holding a wake.

And even in that task, the two brothers were jealous of one another, not so much about the woman as they were about their solicitude for the teacher. When Gesuino—who despite his grumbling and aggressiveness was the weaker of the two— arrived, a wordless clash would take place on the doorstep. Proto looked at him menacingly, pushing him back, and only the realization that the teacher was watching prevented him from seriously sending his brother away.

Gesuino would enter in triumph, and Proto left in anger, determined never to return.

Towards dawn the rain stopped, and in the great, abrupt silence, the rooster's crow seemed the harbinger of a mysterious being arrived from afar to bring peace to the troubled scene.

Even Ornella had nodded off. The teacher covered her with his coat and put a new candle on the holder. A good part of the old one had melted into a cluster of white teardrops, while the new one gave off a sweet, serene little flame that only seemed to flicker when the rooster's second crow penetrated like a sunbeam through the narrow window of the loft.

The teacher went back down and prepared the coffee while Gesuino dozed next to the fireplace like a dog that's listening despite being asleep.

The teacher listened as well. He felt like he'd never been sleepy, but had still slept a long time despite himself. And in the silence he heard a vague creaking outside, as if the night were cracking to let the daylight through, and things bowed by the storm lifted up trembling, while bushes, beach reeds, and mushroom umbrellas emerged from the watery veil covering the earth like treetops after the Great Flood.

This sensation of being saved from a cataclysm, and like Noah in his ark, having the seed of a new humanity saved along with him, never left him again. And he felt like he was still sailing, on a sea more merciless than the real sea, but the hope of making landfall was so strong that he didn't even need to repeat the old sailor's song invoking the Lord, since the

Lord was present there, within his conscience, his strength, and especially in his will to overcome.

The rooster's third crow marked the silent arrival, on bicycle, of the little midwife.

70.

Tiny and very young, she would've passed for a little girl, except for her furrowed brow and two tired, heavily shadowed, black eyes that seemed to have gathered up all the sleeplessness she'd ever experienced.

As she set the bicycle down outside the door, she cast a skeptical glance into the room, at first thinking someone had played a joke on her. Then she saw the stairs, and without further ado removed her cloak, under which she was still wearing the white tunic she used when assisting deliveries, and climbed like a squirrel up to the loft.

The teacher was apprehensive about following her. That little woman who'd arrived silent as a white bird with black wings aroused in him a sense of mystery, and at the same time reminded him of the cruelest reality.

Indeed, he heard her wake Ornella from her dangerous drowsiness, and with a coarse, masculine voice, made her undress and lie supine on the bed. Then she appeared at the top of the staircase and ordered:

"Hot water, hurry."

The teacher thought about putting the pot on the stove, but Gesuino was faster. He stoked the fire and hung the small copper cauldron full of water on the hook of the chain dangling above.

"We have to make a nice polenta," he said, entirely pleased and proud of his witty remark.

Even the teacher smiled and perked up. And to have an excuse to go up and take a look, he considered bringing the midwife a cup of boiling coffee with a lot of sugar.

71.

The baby was born at sunrise. In fact, the sun was already sending its rays through the narrow window whose glass was sparkling like a prism.

"It's a boy," announced the midwife. Due to its large size, it had nearly suffocated during birth and wasn't crying. The baby looked dead with the umbilical cord attached to his bloody, bluish body. She grabbed him by the feet, head down, and gave him a disdainful smack on the buttocks, as if he'd already committed a sin.

Then a sort of roar filled the silence and filled the house with wonder. It was the baby awaking to life.

With an agile hand, as if playing with a toy, the midwife turned him right-side up again, wrapped him in a warm cloth, and quickly passed him to the teacher's arms.

"That's right. Now let's tend to the mother."

When the mother was situated and wrapped up, the midwife turned to look for the baby, and saw that the teacher hadn't budged an inch from the spot where she'd handed him the newborn. Perhaps he hadn't even taken a breath, his face filled with amazement and fear, his hands motionless, supporting that strange bundle which was emitting inhuman shrieks and wails.

72.

Gesuino had just set another pot of water to boil, even though it wasn't needed anymore, when Proto returned with a parcel he was trying to conceal.

"Now go home and do what needs to be done," he ordered, scowling at his brother, expecting a protest. To his surprise, Gesuino pointed his index finger at the loft and then brought it to his lips in a gesture of silence. Then he left without a word.

Proto stood there looking up, curious and anxious, imagining that things were still as they were the night before.

In fact, nothing was really different. The midwife had already gone, and a profound silence prevailed over the room and the loft. It felt like the teacher and Ornella had run off, leaving no life in the house save for the fire and the pot of furiously boiling water on it.

Proto, however, wasn't a man easily intimidated. He set his package on the table, but then it occurred to him that since the pot was boiling, he should take advantage of it. So he unwrapped the already well-plucked chicken with its head shoved between its thighs, and after ensuring that the water was clean, he threw it in. Knowing where the salt was kept, he took a handful and tossed it into the pot. Then he regretted it because he knew that it was better to give sick people unsalted broth.

And he began to wait. But the silence continued up there. Finally, he screwed up his courage and climbed the stairs. Frozen, like in a portrait, he saw Ornella asleep, and the teacher sitting on the crate with his folded-up jacket on his lap, covering something that he seemed worried about putting down or breaking. And the round blue window looked like a giant eye with the sun in the middle for a pupil.

73.

Noticing the farmer, the teacher motioned with his head for him to leave and not disturb Ornella's rest. Then he lifted the edge of the coat. He constantly worried about suffocating the baby. Then again, he couldn't put him in the too narrow bed with his mother, and he didn't want to bring him down below.

Waiting for the midwife to return, and now sure that Proto would see to the household chores, he let himself get lost in thought.

The midwife had taken it upon herself to report the baby's birth to the mayor, and even on that point, he was tranquil. Then, in Ornella's bundled things, he'd found enough money to provide for their most pressing expenses. His only wish was that Antonio wouldn't return. Still, his absence, after all that bluster of the prior evening, made his heart ache. But what did it matter? It's all God's will, and now he felt an extraordinary strength that ensured him he could defend, *at all costs*, the little one that fate had entrusted to him.

Even Ornella, who was sleeping with only her squashed braids for a pillow, pale, mouth half-open like a little child who'd fallen asleep, aroused deep compassion in him. It seemed to him that with the blood spilled and the pain suffered, she'd emptied herself of sin and was purified. And she was there, motionless, like a wax statue that he could alter to suit his taste. She'd even lost that heavy breathing of hers, and her forehead and nose had a childlike contour.

And there, all of a sudden, without knowing why, he found himself back in the village school: Five poor children, all ugly and insolent, sitting at their desks, were staring at him derisively.

"Wow," said one of them, the smallest and meanest, "you, Mr. Giuseppe, sir, who couldn't see us, and now you have to be the wet nurse for that mangy little brat."

The others laughed. One of the well-mannered boys, the well-to-do ones, stood and began making atrocious faces.

"Aren't you going to give *me* any milk, Mr. Giuseppe, sir?"

The entire class was struck by an epidemic of smirking and laughter. Some boys threw acorns and rotten olives at him, trying more to hit the baby than him. He tried to stand but couldn't, or rather, wouldn't, and crossed his arms to shield the baby from the attack.

"This is a penance as well," he thought, "since I never loved children."

Suddenly someone climbed up the stairs. In the opening to the loft appeared Ola's beautiful head, with those black curls and golden-brown eyes. He felt himself flush and tried to better conceal the baby, but Ola knew everything. She jumped up into the middle of the loft and said:

"Give me a stick to defend my little brother against those macaques."

The children, however, had vanished, and in place of the school was the sea, with its rough waves. The children had vanished—where? He thought they'd all jumped on his lap, hiding in the folds of the overcoat, which felt heavy and was sliding down. It did slide down, in fact, and the baby slipped out in pieces, all bloodied and bruised.

He awoke terrified from having momentarily nodded off and lifted the edge of the coat once more to ensure that the baby was there, intact. He was there, with his big head in a reddish woolen bonnet. His eyes were wide open, expressionless, and those eyes and his little face, shiny and red as if his outer skin had peeled away, strangely resembled those of Ola's doll.

74.

Antonio returned as well, rigid and unemotional. With his pantlegs tucked into his tall leather boots and holding a riding crop, he looked like a jockey preparing for a dangerous race. In fact, he announced he was leaving on business, as well as for another reason which he only confided to the teacher.

"I'm going to look for a little house to situate Ornella and the baby, as soon as they're able to travel. Until then, here…"

He wanted to give him money. The older man was uncertain whether to take it or not. He took it, but set it aside, like someone determined not to spend someone else's money on himself.

Antonio also wanted to see the baby and Ornella. The midwife, returning for a second time, had arranged things so that the two could share the bed and the mother could nurse her baby.

When Antonio climbed up to the loft, Ornella was, in fact, turned a bit to her side, nursing the baby, giving the physical impression of being completely at one with him. Even though his tender little mouth tenaciously sucking her nipple hurt like he was biting her, it aroused a sense of carnal pleasure, and she thought she never wanted it to detach from her again. And she felt that if someone tried to pull the baby from her breast, she would immediately transform into a wild beast to defend him.

In fact, when Antonio bent over the bed, she remembered his evil plans and her eyes gleamed with hatred.

Antonio, however, had no intention of making an emotional scene. In fact, his indifference towards the mother and son clearly showed on his glowering face. His only concern, for the moment, was for the teacher not to think him stingy and irresponsible, and back downstairs in the room from which Proto had judiciously excused himself, he tried to offer more money.

"No, no," said the teacher, disgustedly pushing away the hand that was offering it. "Enough!"

That *enough* meant other things. Antonio understood and went on to explain:

"Anyway, I'll be back in three or four days and will have found a place to situate them, and if Ornella is in a condition to travel, everything will be over and done."

The teacher didn't answer, and when Antonio had gone, he recalled the last time he'd seen him before he ran away from home as a boy. "A moment earlier he'd been eating my bread and drinking my wine, and then he left without even giving me a look of compassion. But it's right that everything is this way," he thought, going back up to see Ornella.

He found her red and agitated, with terror in her eyes.

"What did he tell you?" she demanded, her voice loud and mistrustful.

"Nothing. He told me nothing."

"No, no, I know what he intends—he wants to kill the baby!"

"You're crazy, Ornella. What's gotten into you?"

"It's the truth, I'm telling you. You'll see. And last night, didn't he want to kill me? Along with the baby? *And that first time?*"

"Hush, don't get upset, don't think about anything. It'll dry up your milk."

But Ornella wouldn't listen to reason, terrified like a bird that's seen a red kite pass by.

"You'll see, you'll see. He wanted to take me away so he could make the baby disappear. And that's still what he'll do, unless…"

"Unless?"

"Unless I run away. That's the other reason I wanted to go away with Bianchi. He's a thousand times better than that murderer here."

"Ornella!" said the teacher, disheartened and distressed. "Don't say bad words. Now you have a son listening."

She looked at the baby as if he really was listening to her. She pouted, seemingly on the verge of tears.

Then to calm her, the teacher put his hand on her head and pronounced some strange words, almost without realizing it. They were the Bible verses that spoke of Herod's persecution:

"An angel of the Lord appeared to Joseph in a dream, saying, 'Arise, take the young child and his mother, flee to Egypt, and stay there until I bring you word, for Herod will seek the young child to kill him.' So he arose, took the young child and his mother by night, and fled into Egypt."

Ornella understood what he meant perfectly, and just like that frightened bird that finds a cranny in which to hide, she calmed down and resumed nursing her baby.

75.

The one who proved most useful under the circumstances was Gesuino.

He washed the newborn's diapers, dealt with the household chores, and, to not appear inferior to his brother, also brought a gift: a fine hunk of pork, encased in fat.

"I want to roast this one my own special way, so that Ornella will be licking her fingers."

"To me it seems a bit early to feed her pork," the teacher observed good-naturedly, and to not offend Gesuino, he added: "Instead, let's have a little feast for ourselves."

And that's what they did. That evening Proto went to buy wine to "wash down" the roast (which was actually cooked to perfection with rosemary and bay leaves), but also, as he and the host were well aware, for the teacher to drink after many long years of abstinence. And drink he did. And naturally, he got drunk. But it was a conscious, voluntary drunkenness that made him feel like he was taking his soul out for a walk on a fine summer morning, letting it flutter about here and there like butterflies in the meadows along the seashore, keeping an eye on it, however, so it wouldn't run into danger.

And so he restrained his desire to tell the farmers his plans for the future. Besides, even they were hardly talking that night, to avoid disturbing Ornella. There was some racket, however, when the little midwife arrived and after she'd settled the new mother and baby for the night.

"Have a glass with us," invited the teacher. She didn't need to be asked twice. "I have things to do tonight, and I don't want to fall in a ditch," she said with her coarse voice, downing the wine in one gulp, like tossing it out the window.

"One for me too," Proto said gallantly, standing up and handing her a full glass.

"Oh well," she replied, taking the glass in her tiny hands as if trying to warm them up or warm up the wine. "This is really going to hit me hard."

Then Gesuino raised his big head whose curly-haired shadow fluttered on the wall like that of a thorny tree and pronounced his verdict:

"To keep wine from hitting you hard, you must drink *three* glasses of it."

"Sure! In the name of the Father, the Son, and the Holy Ghost."

"Amen," the farmer replied earnestly, offering his full glass as well. "If you don't drink, I'll be offended."

"You know what?" interrupted the teacher, concerned about the midwife's safety. "To keep wine from hitting you, you need to eat something. Have a seat."

"I have things to do, I told you!" shouted the woman. But Proto stood, grabbed her by the shoulders and forced her to sit down. The teacher put a slice of the roast, some bread, and salt in front of her, and she stayed there until late in the night.

They spoke softly, and she told stories about all the families in town, with crude details and expressions that equaled anything Ornella had ever said in her worst moments. In the dark, one would have mistaken her for an uncouth boy of the worst sort. Even so, the teacher, and even Gesuino who, like Frate Zappata, never practiced what he preached, not only felt sorry for her, but listened to her with perverse pleasure.

Proto, on the other hand, was getting irritated, and to put a stop to her scandalmongering, he wanted to tell some of his old stories.

"Well, once time in a little village in the middle of nowhere was a parish priest who couldn't stand being alone. And so one evening he sent a servant with the cart to beg the doctor to come right away because he was feeling ill. The doctor, who was an old friend anyway, arrived. 'Well, then, how are you doing? What's wrong?' 'What's wrong,' said the priest, 'is that I feel like I'm dying. I have a great pain here, at the top of my head, and also here, at the tip of my elbow, and then here, at the tip of my toe. Then, at night when I put out the light, I can't see anymore.' 'Oh, son of a bitch!" shouted the doctor. Then he stayed for dinner with the priest and at midnight they were still playing cards and drinking."

Everyone laughed, although the teacher thought he'd heard that story other times before. When the midwife had finally gone, he climbed up to the loft to see if the racket had disturbed Ornella. In fact, she was lying there with her eyes open because she tried not to fall asleep at night out of fear of suffocating the baby.

"We celebrated his birth," the teacher mumbled, leaning over the bed that smelled of straw and milk like a manger. "Those good-natured farmers brought some gifts."

"Why not show them the baby?" she asked, with a sleepy, dreamy voice that reminded him of Marga's. "He's so handsome. He's already smiling. He's so big and handsome," she repeated with an air of pride.

"Tomorrow."

"Why not now? He's even more handsome at night," she insisted, fondling the baby, all warm and moist with milk.

The teacher was still in a state of slight drunkenness that made everything seem easy and wonderful. So he stuck his head through the opening in the loft floor and called the farmers.

"Ornella wants to show you the baby."

They came up the steps, first Gesuino, quickly, and then Proto, more pensively. Then the two approached and looked.

"Handsome, truly handsome. He must weigh about ten or eleven pounds," said Proto. "He looks like a fat piglet."

Rather than offending Ornella, the comparison pleased her. And as he stood there in front of the little bed that smelled of straw and milk, the teacher thought he saw in himself and the farmers the three Wise Men admiring the baby Jesus.

Part V

———◆◇◆———

The Flight

76.

The third day after the delivery, Ornella declared that she wanted to get up. She felt perfectly fine, stronger because she was more agile than before.

"I have to go out for a few hours. It's best if you stay in bed, in case Antonio should come," the teacher advised.

She immediately understood and didn't insist. It seemed that after the baby was born, her intelligence had expanded in an extraordinary way.

The teacher asked Gesuino to keep an eye on the house while he was away, and so the farmer went to settle into the room, bringing along a broken basin he wanted to fix with a needle, wire, and glue.

The teacher had never been superstitious, and yet, seeing the basin in two pieces, green on the inside and red on the outside, and hearing Gesuino's plan to put it back together, he thought:

"If the basin is successfully repaired when I return, it means that my business will be successful as well."

He went to the nearby town where the magistrate resided to officially surrender custody of the sequestered house. He went on foot, along the seashore.

The weather had completely cleared. It was cold, but a dry cold, and the sea, beneath a crystalline blue sky, seemed to quiver with delight at having regained the transparency and splendor of its tranquil days. The sand was untouched, and the teacher was almost apprehensive about violating it with his footprints. The memory of Ola assailed him from time to time with impassioned brutality, as if she herself with her spirited, determined little body were unexpectedly jumping onto his neck. But almost like a guilty thought, he pushed it away.

The path was a different one, now, well-marked and without playful stops. And it was long, as long as the rest of his life. And so he needed to hurry. And hurry he did. Down below, the bright, smiling town seemed to approach him to offer its assistance. Even the sand turned hard under his feet, and the entire beach, gray and golden, resembled a broad avenue along the blue garden of the sea.

77.

He returned on the train, bearing a package of cookies for Ornella.

Gesuino was still there, sweeping in front of the house.

"The basin?" asked the teacher.

"Oh, I broke it," said the farmer, but his eyes brimmed with a mischievous gleam. In fact, the basin was inside, on fine display on the table, clean and intact like it had just come from the store. Curious, the teacher walked around it, almost suspecting a hoax. Then he began laughing like a little boy.

"Very well then!" he exclaimed, taking off his overcoat with a youthful deftness. "No one came?"

"Only that bane of a midwife, and she nearly beat me because the hot water wasn't ready. But she's good, whew! She did everything in two minutes."

"Did you give Ornella something?"

Gesuino hesitated before responding, but he was a scrupulous man who didn't care for telling lies.

"I wanted to give her a cup of broth like you suggested, but the girl began yawning and making faces. She said, 'Of course I'm hungry, with this parasite sucking my blood!' Then she told me to give her bread with a wedge of pig fat, and she wouldn't take no for an answer."

"Let's hope nothing happens," the teacher said, alarmed, and he went up with the cookies, expecting to receive a prompt expression of gratitude from Ornella. She was sitting on the bed yawning so much she had to squeeze her cheeks with her open hand. Taking the cookies, she said:

"These will be good for the baby. I want pasta and beans."

78.

That hunger that the teacher attempted to satisfy as best he could with less vulgar foods than the ones Ornella wanted, had its effects. On the fourth day she got up and combed her hair, screaming in pain from how tangled it had become, and then she went downstairs to reclaim the reins of household management. Sometimes, though, she pricked up her ears, and if she thought she heard a familiar stride, she would dart up to the loft to hide away and protect her little one.

Her hatred for Antonio caused her to exaggerate the danger—it was as if he really had fired his revolver at her and the unborn baby—the terror lingered in her blood, and she couldn't think clearly enough to overcome it.

The evening of the fifth day, then, while Antonio still hadn't turned up, Proto brought the news that Adelmo Bianchi, the parricide, had been found and captured in Genoa as he was attempting to board a ship for America.

Ornella seemed to take in the news with indifference, but when the farmer had left, she said with vehemence:

"It was him, *Antonio*, spying and—"

The teacher didn't let her continue, more outraged than she'd ever seen him before.

"I forbid you to slander Antonio this way, do you understand?"

As it turned out, the next day things appeared different: Adelmo Bianchi had turned himself in spontaneously.

"Maybe he learned that I'd delivered and could no longer join him," Ornella said, without conceit. And the teacher, pleased by her confession, thought it best to leave her with her illusion. Proto, however, had already told him that Bianchi had turned himself in because his brother, in prison, was threatening to hang himself if they continued postponing the trial.

79.

This terrible drama's epilogue, and a very simple thing that occurred that same day, solidified the teacher's conviction that everything proceeded according to the hand of God.

During that time, the owner to whom he had sold his house with a repurchase option had died, and his son wrote that the family wouldn't challenge the agreement. However, the former owner's presence was required for the transfer to legally proceed.

He showed the letter to Ornella.

"The transaction could also be carried out by proxy," he said, taking back the letter and looking at it to avoid looking at the woman. "That's too expensive, though. I'm planning on going down there in person. I've already arranged for the magistrate to send a new caretaker here as soon as possible. The minute he arrives, I'll hand everything over to him and leave."

"What about me? And the baby?"

He looked up, already rather hesitant.

"If you want to come, with the baby, we'll leave together."

"And you just assumed I'll go?" she asked indignantly.

"All right. Listen to me, then, Ornella. You'll come with me and be whatever you want to be. To be clear, though, I'm going to consider the baby as my own son. Once we're down there, I'll arrange everything. We'll baptize him and make him legitimate. And he must grow up with the certainty that he really is my son. I'll continue to work, for the two of you; I feel I have the strength for it. One more thing: we need to leave here in secret, to avoid nosy people. We'll take the train from the next station. All right?"

"All right," she answered, and they didn't talk anymore.

The teacher decided not to involve the farmers in his and Ornella's flight. They would consider him an ingrate, but if a man wants a secret kept, he must start with keeping it to himself.

Besides, circumstances seemed to mysteriously favor him. The new caretaker, accompanied by an agent of the court whom the teacher already knew, arrived one evening when the farmers were away.

Everything was ready for their departure, and once the main house and the caretaker's residence had been turned over, there was nothing left for the teacher to do but leave.

He'd packed up his and Ornella's things in the two suitcases with which he'd arrived. He removed the little tapestry of *The Flight into Egypt*, rolled it up, and wrapped it in a sheet of tissue paper. When he and Ornella, holding the baby covered in her shawl, passed by the farmers' house, he shoved the roll inside through a broken window pane.

They knew the value of the gift and would understand its meaning.

Then he and Ornella walked along the beach, in the gray night illuminated by the big winter stars, with the baby who was the only one not to leave any footprints behind.

From the Translator's Notebook

First, this section is hardly essential in order to read and enjoy Deledda's novel; in fact, this motley collection of notes and comments will likely interest very few—perhaps mostly those who enjoy reading about language and translation in general.

I do want to explicitly state that I took on this project of translating *The Flight into Egypt* with the realization that my English version would thus become *the* representation of Deledda's novel to many English speakers, and I didn't take that responsibility lightly. Striving to capture her voice, rhythm, and tone and faithfully render it in an English that feels natural to the reader, I often found myself asking: *If Deledda had been writing in English rather than Italian, how would she have said this?*

One thing to keep in mind is that when Deledda wrote, she wasn't using "old-fashioned" language, nor did her readers perceive it as such. Therefore, I wanted to make the English translation sound reasonably modern (as Deledda's Italian did to her readers at the time), resisting any temptation to fill the book with antiquated, excessively formal, or painfully stilted prose (even if some of Deledda's words and turns of phrases may now be considered "literary" and sound odd or quaint to today's Italian reader). At the same time, however,

I deemed it important to remain faithful to the time period, avoiding anachronistic words and phrases, ones that didn't exist or weren't used in English when the book was originally published. These parallel guidelines led me to the path of a neutral, timeless American English (which is more of a concept than an actual reality). To that end, I am indebted to references such as the online Etymology Dictionary which I consulted frequently (and was frequently surprised to learn that particular words or phrases which I suspected might be too modern had in fact entered the English language centuries ago).

My main goal, however, was to represent Deledda well with a natural, readable, and enjoyable English translation. I'll leave it to others to determine the extent of my success (or failure) in that endeavor.

A few general notes about *The Flight into Egypt:*

The original book mainly narrates in the past tense, but multiple passages, long and short, are written in the present tense, with shifts between past and present popping up seemingly at random, sometimes within a single paragraph. The use of the "historical present" isn't all that odd in Italian (it's also sometimes found in English), but I felt it would seem more natural—less jarring, certainly—to maintain a consistent use of (past) tense throughout the narration.

As for the chapters, I've added numbers which don't appear in the public domain scans of the original 1926 edition published by "Fratelli Treves, Editori" in Milan. Instead, the text was divided by a symbol (somewhat resembling a squashed spider) centered in a blank space roughly five print lines tall. I simply considered each of these divisions to be a chapter break. The resulting 79 chapters (many less than a page long) may seem a lot, but the author clearly intended her work to be so divided, and the result is eminently readable and oddly modern. Further, for formatting and structural purposes, I broke the book down into five "parts" that don't appear in the original work, with titles of my own creation. (Many contemporary ebook formats recommend or even require a table of contents with hyperlinks to chapters, but a TOC with 79 chapters seemed excessive and pointless. Breaking the book into parts solved this problem.) At any rate, purists can simply ignore the parts.

While adopting contemporary English punctuation practices, I've maintained the author's original paragraphs almost entirely. On perhaps fewer than a dozen occasions, I joined or divided paragraphs when it seemed important to add clarity or enhance narrative flow. Of note, Deledda almost always places dialogue at the start of a new paragraph, even if it results in two single-line paragraphs (one a brief sentence about the character or his/her actions, the next the same character's dialogue) that would almost certainly be written as one paragraph in contemporary English style. I carried her practice over to the translation with rare exception.

Many of Deledda's sentences begin with (the Italian equivalent of) "And" or "And so" or "And thus." Occasionally

I slightly reworked a sentence to better conform to "standard" English grammar and to provide some relief from a frequently repeated sentence pattern, but I quite often carried over her structure, even though at times it might look a bit unconventional (or even ungrammatical) to some. In my (and Deledda's) defense, I found numerous examples of sentences beginning "And so" in literature all the way back to Shakespeare. Here's an example from *Hamlet*: "And now I'll do't. And so he goes to heaven. And so am I revenged."

Character names: I haven't altered any names in any way. Of note, Marga talks about her first husband, Adelmo (first mentioned in chapter 4). Then, in chapter 54, we meet an entirely different character, Adelmo Bianchi, the father-killer (*parricide* is a fancy word for one who kills a parent, and the closest word to the Italian one Deledda used, but I deemed it too rare and too awkward in English to use more than a few times). I honestly found this recycling of the name "Adelmo" a bit confusing at first, and I'm not sure why Deledda chose to use the same first name for two different characters. Any intended symbolic link between the two men is lost on me. (Should any readers have any thoughts, feel free to email me!)

Speaking of characters' names, in Chapter 11, Ola mentions "Gina Bluvin," while in chapter 15, Ornella talks about a woman (of ill repute, according to Ornella!) named "Bulvin." I suspect they are one in the same, and some sort of typo explains the discrepancy. As these are the only two references to the character(s) in the book, and the exact spelling is inconsequential to the story, I simply left the names as they appeared in the scans of the original 1926 edition.

Now I'll turn to a few specific matters (translation choices and cultural notes) that arose, addressing them in order of appearance.

Far from a comprehensive list (which would entail a volume unto itself) of all the choices I made in translating, all the odd or fascinating turns of phrases in Deledda's original that presented intriguing challenges, I've included only a few representative ones here, hopefully those of broadest appeal.

Chapter 8

Cominciò col dargli del voi.

Literally: He began by addressing him with *Voi* (rather than the *Lei* form of "you").

Here, Antonio shifted from a more formal *Lei* to *Voi* (while his father has been addressing him as *tu*). Thus, Antonio (supposedly) begins addressing him more as an equal, yet not with the same informality or familiarity as his father uses with him. (Interestingly, Antonio used the *Voi* form only twice in that chapter before addressing his father with *Lei* again for the entire remainder of the book.)

Background:

In Italian, there are basically three different ways to say "you"—*tu*, *Voi*, and *Lei*. (To be complete, there is also a rare, antiquated *Loro*!)

Children address their parents with *tu*, so it sounds a bit odd (overly formal) to me for Antonio to address his father as *Lei* while his father was using *tu*. In fact, even the *Voi* sounds odd from a contemporary perspective. (Although addressing family members as *Voi* isn't really strange from a historical perspective: in Federico De Roberto's highly recommended classic novel *I Viceré* (1894), *Voi* was the common mode of address among the noble Uzeda family members in Sicily.)

In modern, standard Italian, *voi* is mostly reserved for *you* in the plural, that is, for addressing a group (or the public in official/legal documents or settings). Italians today use *voi* where we would say "you guys" (which is one of several English workarounds to our lack of a plural second-person address). Historically, as I mentioned, and still in some regions, particularly among older individuals in smaller towns toward the south of the peninsula, *Voi* might still be used in place of *Lei* to address a single person somewhat formally.

Of course, that's a bit of an oversimplification. Clearly, it's a complex topic, particularly for speakers of English with only one *you* to deal with! So, to keep the story flowing and avoid a lengthy grammatical explanation or awkward discussion (that's what this section is for!), I chose to paraphrase that Italian sentence for the English version, fully realizing that this would be a clear case of something "being lost in translation," and for that I apologize.

This explanation hopefully serves to restore, at least in part, that lost nuance. If the subject is of interest to you, the

Wikipedia article "T-V Distinction" can get you started with more information, including a fascinating table of languages showing their various methods of addressing "you."

Chapter 9

Early in the chapter, Marga is described as constantly criticizing Ornella who accepted it impassively, like a statue. Five short paragraphs later, the cat is described as waiting for Ornella to return from shopping. Those intervening paragraphs don't give the impression of much time passing, so this is a slightly jolting turn. (I thought: *Wait, wasn't Ornella just standing right there?*)

Chapter 10

C'è il gatto mammone? — lei domandò messa un po' in terrore da tutta quella grandezza sconosciuta.

The *Gatto Mammone*, (Mammon Cat) is an interesting mythical creature, and folklore surrounding the *Gatto* has been told up and down the entire Italian peninsula (and beyond, in Goethe's *Faust*, for example).

As with any folklore, there are countless, often contradictory, tales and myths in circulation. For those interested, the Italian Wikipedia article "Gatto mammone" provides a nice starting point for those who can read some Italian.

Here, however, is one brief story:

A mother sends her beautiful daughter to an enchanted castle to ask the fairies for a favor. The girl sees the palace cats doing chores, washing and cleaning. Being a kind, helpful sort, she assists them with their work. In return, their leader, the *Gatto Mammone*, tells the girl a secret: On her way home, she mustn't turn her head when she hears a donkey braying. She obeys and is rewarded with a beautiful glowing star on her forehead. Her sister, envious of this adornment, goes to the castle as well, but ignores the cats and refuses to help them, so the *Gatto* doesn't share this crucial secret with her. Of course, when the sister heads home, the donkey brays, she turns, and instead of a glowing star, she ends up with a donkey's tail in the middle of her forehead! The moral of the story? Never be mean to a cat, especially not the *Gatto Mammone*!

Chapter 12

— *Va là, in fatto di studio sei una zuccona come tuo padre,* — *prese un pezzetto di zucca e glielo mise sotto il guanciale; e quando lui protestò, rispose:*

— *È un pezzo della mia testa.*

A play on words. A *zucca* is literally a gourd, squash, or pumpkin. It can also refer to a person's head. (Not unlike English, when we say someone is out of their gourd.) *Zuccone* (or here, the feminine version *zuccona*) in this case refers to an obtuse person, and we have a wealth of choices in English: dolt, dope, idiot, dunce, numbskull, bonehead, chump, nitwit, lummox, etc. I elected to use "blockhead" so I could replicate the joke.

In Italian, the teacher called Ola a *zuccona*, so she stuck a piece of a *zucca* under his pillow, saying it was a piece of her head.

In English, the teacher calls her a blockhead, so she sticks a piece of wood under his pillow as the piece of her head.

Chapter 15

— *In bestia non puoi andare, perché bestia tu sei già, porco e traditore.*

Here's an example of a little wordplay that I think suffers somewhat in the English. *Andare in bestia* (literally "to go in beast") means to lose one's temper/get mad/fly off the handle. Meanwhile, *bestia* can also figuratively refer to a person who is a "beast" or "animal" or "brute" (as in English).

She's saying he can't "go in beast" because he already *is* a beast. (It's somewhat like the old line: "You can't drive me crazy because I'm already there.") Then to clarify, she adds that's he's a "pig" and a "two-timer" (a cheater or traitor). I had to massage the dialogue a bit to find a natural way to fit all the elements in.

Chapter 16

— *Tutti siamo impastati di bene e di male, ma quest'ultimo bisogna vincerlo, Antonio. L'acciaio che è l'acciaio viene temprato e ridotto a spada, da chi vuol vincere il nemico.*

"We're all awash in good and evil, but the latter must be defeated, Antonio. Steel—even steel—can be tempered and forged into a sword by those wishing to vanquish their enemy."

Not much to say here, except the meaning of this sentence somewhat eluded me when I first read it, and I'm not sure why. I'd like to take this opportunity to give a shout out to Bernardo, a thoughtful native speaker who took the time to explain this sentence to me in Italian. Incredibly, after reading his Italian paraphrase of the sentence in question, it all seemed so clear that I wondered why it had ever given me any trouble! Needless to say, I'm incredibly grateful for this and other explanations he graciously provided which contributed to improving my translation!

Since I found the original quote on a several Italian websites, I spent a good deal of effort on the translation. Although I've captured the meaning, and I do like the English sentence, I'm not entirely convinced that it matches the original in elegance and literary punch.

Chapter 26

I used the expression to have something "in spades." This is attested in print as early as 1929, so perhaps it represents the rare anachronism in the translation of a book originally published in 1926 (I say "perhaps" because it's likely that the phrase had been used in speech prior to when it is first known to have appeared in print). However, the tone of the phrase seemed perfect for the character and situation, so I made the rare exception of letting this slip by. To my knowledge, it's the only anachronistic word or phrase I used, and I checked literally hundreds.

Chapter 55

The story references a place called "Isole Rosse":

— Non lo so neppure io: ho tutta una confusione in mente. Dapprima sono stato giù, verso le Isole Rosse, in una specie di grotta marina che pochi conoscono.

I couldn't find anything with the current name of "Isole Rosse" (Red Isles/Islands), but a well-known town/beach area on the northern tip of Sardinia called "Isola Rossa" (Red Isle/Island) fits the description and context of the novel. (I added the "Sardinia" reference as unobtrusively as possible to the translated dialogue for the benefit of Anglophone readers, most of whom likely aren't familiar with Isola Rossa.)

Chapter 56

Laggiù dove voglio andare potrò forse anche arrolarmi nelle **milizie coloniali**,...

For *milizia coloniale* I simply used "colonial militia." Undoubtedly, the original held more meaning for the Italian reader then than the translation will for most Anglophone readers now, but I didn't want to encumber the novel by inserting political and/or historical context of dubious importance to the story, and so, I'll chalk this up as another example of some nuance lost in translation.

Here, however, from Wikipedia is a bit of background: "The **Milizia Coloniale** was an all-volunteer colonial militia composed of members of the Fascist *Milizia Volontaria per la Sicurezza Nazionale* ("Volunteer Militia for National Security") or MVSN, commonly called the "Blackshirts." It is considered unique in modern Italian military history, with its reputation matched only by the pre-unification paramilitary forces Redshirts."

Chapter 59

Col suo pastrano giallognolo guarnito di pelo, un berretto pure di pelo calato come una cuffia intorno al viso rosso, così corrucciato com'era, egli dava l'idea di un esquimese selvaggio.

Obviously, in 2020, using "Eskimo" in this context is insulting (*exoticism* comes to mind). When Deledda wrote this in the 1920s, the world was of course very different, and I have no reason to suspect that she meant any offense or disrespect to Innuit peoples who surely must have seemed distant and exotic to her. My work here is as a translator, and so it's not my place to "correct" or "edit" Deledda (or bring her up-to-date with 21st century norms!), so I chose not to alter or omit this phrase.

On that subject, briefly turning back to Chapter 14, the character of the old woman refers to that *paese di ebrei* (lit. town of Jews), and the teacher mentally comments about how the residents there were "perhaps a little too attached to it [money] in fact, like Israelite merchants." Again, although recognizing the offensive nature of the stereotypes conveyed, I elected to translate rather than to edit or censor. After all, the fact that people's knowledge and perceptions of others were different a hundred years ago is hardly surprising, and one of the reasons we read classic literature is to see how people lived and thought in the past, and so hiding or disguising these references would ultimately be a disservice to today's readers.

Chapter 63

> — *E poi provvedere a loro: chi ha rotto paga.*

An interesting line. Literally: "And then provide for them: he who broke (it) pays."

The first thing that came to mind was "You break it, you buy it!"—a common cliché. It sounded too modern to my ear, and in fact, some sources say it first appeared in 1952. So I compromised with: "If you break it, you pay for it" which is closer to the original. It still sounds almost too modern to me, but obviously none of the words is anachronistic and the sentence and thought could just as easily have been uttered in English in 1926 as it was in Italian.

Chapter 72

Here the little window in the loft is described as "round" (*finestrino rotondo*) like "a big eye." However, in chapter 68, the window is described as *finestrino simile a una feritoia* (a little window similar to an embrasure or a slit).

Chapter 75

Frate Zappata is mentioned. I couldn't find much about him, but his name does appear in at least one list of proverbs/sayings:

Far come padre Zappata che predicava bene e razzolava male is listed as an Italian turn of phrase/figure of speech referring to someone who advises others to be honest but doesn't behave that way himself. (*Di chi dà consigli d'onestà ma onestamente non si comporta.*)

In other words, doing like Friar or Father Zappata means not practicing what you preach.

About the Translator / Other Books Available

Kevan Houser began studying Italian independently in the 1970s as a high school student and continued a more traditional study at the University of Oregon, including a stint as an exchange student in Perugia, Italy, finally receiving his BA in Italian from San Francisco State University in 1994.

He now lives in Portland, and besides gainful work as a commercial/business translator, he has translated several genre novels and shorter fiction, providing an American voice for self-published Italian authors.

Besides publishing his own well-received thriller, *Karma's Envoy*, he's been working diligently to bring other Italian classics (including more by Grazia Deledda) back into the spotlight with fresh, modern translations!

You can reach him at: envoyfeedback@yahoo.com

Here are some other classic translations now available:

Elias Portolu by Grazia Deledda

Returning to his Sardinia home after a stint in a prison on the Italian mainland, young Elias desperately wants to be an obedient son, a hard-working shepherd, and a loyal brother, and his initial progress in that direction raises his devout mother's hopes that her youngest boy is back on the path of righteousness.

But when Elias falls in love with the wrong woman, he quickly finds himself battling sin, and is willing to go to any length to overcome it.

Deledda poignantly unfolds the tale of a fundamentally tortured soul, a young man torn between good and evil, between being a man of God or a mortal man with desires of the flesh, between his duty to his family and his only chance at happiness.

Elias Portolu is a fascinating glimpse into a vanished world of modest, humble, hard-working Sardinian shepherds and farmers enjoying life as they eke out an existence on the sometimes harsh but always beautiful Mediterranean island at the turn of the twentieth century.

First published in 1903, *Elias Portolu* continues to resonate with readers today because Deledda's crisp, direct prose tells an engaging story that doesn't seem outdated in either theme or style.

Before there was Elena Ferrante, Natalia Ginzburg, or Elsa Morante, **Grazia Deledda** was a prolific writer who received the Nobel Prize for Literature in 1926 (one of only six Italians, and the only Italian woman, to date, to receive this prestigious award).

Now, this early novel is readily available in a fresh, modern English translation, now available in paperback and Kindle editions.

The Amulet by Neera

Fans of **Grazia Deledda** might enjoy this newly translated (2019) short novel by **Neera** (the pen name of Anna Radius Zuccari), one of the most prolific and successful writers of late-nineteenth-century Italy and another classic female voice worthy of rediscovery.

Check out her intriguing novella *The Amulet,* now available as an Amazon Kindle ebook.

A young soldier in a distant land. Memories of his mother, far away and alone. A mysterious, dark-eyed old man. A mysterious amulet. And a handwritten love story…

A young woman's secluded life takes an abrupt turn when her new neighbor, a handsome, young, worldly cousin comes to pay her an introductory visit. Although she is married with a six-year-old son, her husband permanently lives far away, so the woman enjoys her cousin's company and conversation immeasurably, although he's not particularly kind or gracious with her.

Introspective and languid at times, this poetic first-person account from the woman's point of view provides great insight into the psyche of a modest *fin de siècle* Italian wife and mother as her life forever changes.

Beautifully written, fans of Victorian romance and Jane Austin are sure to appreciate this undiscovered gem of classic Italian literature by the prolific woman writer **Neera**.

One, No One & 100,000 by Luigi Pirandello

Luigi Pirandello (1867-1936), world-renowned writer, is arguably best known in the US as a dramatist, particularly for the innovative "theatre within the theatre" aspect of his 1926 *Six Characters in Search of an Author* (*Sei personaggi in cerca d'autore*), which has been called a "technical tour de force" and is still considered an avant-garde masterpiece.

Rather prolific, Pirandello produced hundreds of short stories, several novels, and much poetry in addition to about 50 plays. He was awarded the 1934 Nobel Prize in Literature for "his almost magical power to turn psychological analysis into good theater." (He was also quite capable of turning psychological analysis into good prose, I might add.)

There are at least three readily available English translations of Luigi Pirandello's *One, No One & 100,000*. This engaging, new (2018) version, available on Amazon in Kindle ebook and paperback editions, is the clearest, most direct, most readable one yet.

Countess Baby by Gerolamo Rovetta

Discover another "lost" treasure of Italian literature! **Gerolamo Rovetta's** *Countess Baby* (original title: *Baby*) is the newly translated (2018) romantic novella set in the upper echelons of Verona's high society in the late 1800s. Amazon Kindle ebook edition now available._

A prolific, popular writer at the start of the 20th century, Gerolamo Rovetta has been all but forgotten, particularly in the English-speaking world where his work isn't available in translation.

Now, for quite possibly the first time, you can read Rovetta in English.

Countess Baby (original title: *Baby*) is a romantic novella set in the upper echelons of Verona's high society in the late 1800s. The protagonist is a complex young man, Count Andrea of Santisillia, whose return to Verona after a ten-year absence shakes up the upper echelon of that city's nobility as they vie for the honor of hosting this mysterious loner who fled the city after the tragic death of a chaste love affair.

A man of passion and reflection, he falls in love with a beautiful girl without even caring to know her name, after only exchanging a few weekly glances at mass. She turns out to be his distant cousin, a countess whose petite form and childlike charm earn her the nickname "Baby," and his passion gradually sends him into spiral of madness.

This novella comes with a healthy dose of melodrama, a hint of pessimism, flowery romantic language, chivalry, a touch of humor, and even an old-fashioned duel!

Karma's Envoy by Kevan Houser

Along with translation, Houser enjoys telling original stories. His first original novel, *Karma's Envoy*, has received overwhelmingly positive reviews and is available in paperback and Kindle ebook._

"A promising first novel featuring an unlikely hero."
— *Kirkus Reviews*

"Grabs you from the very start and is genuinely hard to put down." — *HUGEOrange Publication Review*

"Sardonic, sympathetic, harrowing, amusing, and more. A unique and multi-layered novel." — *SPR*

Karma's Envoy: A boy was murdered 50 years ago. Is it too late to save him?

Todd Woodside's entire San Francisco life suddenly disappears when he becomes an 8-year-old boy living in rural Oregon in 1962. Is he dreaming? Dead? Crazy?

His new, chain-smoking mom calls him "Peter" as she fusses to get him ready for school. He soon learns she's also a mentally unstable new widow, making her particularly vulnerable when Jack Quinn, a young local man with a shady past, steps in. When Jack first begins romancing her, Peter doesn't realize the danger they're in and the harrowing life-and-death struggle he will soon face.

How can a little kid protect his fragile mother and defend himself? Will knowledge and experience from his original, future life be enough to save him from a horrific death?

Karma's Envoy blends suspense, mystery, and ironic humor in a unique, time-traveling journey of crime and punishment that lingers long after the book is done.

Here's a sample of what readers are saying about *Karma's Envoy*, the compelling genre-bending psychological thriller now available on Amazon Kindle, Kindle Unlimited, and in paperback:

"I was instantly intrigued and pulled into this story."

"This mesmerizing story is so polished that it seems unlikely it is a first novel."

"What a great book! What a gripping story! You really can't put this book down."

"You won't be able to put this book down, because with every word you'll be wanting to know what happens next."

"Full of suspense with an insanely interesting plot."

"Interesting and complex plot that holds your imagination right to the end."

"A mash up of two genres—crime thriller and time-traveling fantasy (…) a fantastic mix."

"A perfectly written and crafted story."

"The twists and turns kept me wanting to read."

Check out the reviews on Amazon and Goodreads!

Made in the USA
Coppell, TX
11 September 2022